This Life She's Chosen

This Life She's Chosen

stories

Kirsten Sundberg Lunstrum

CHRONICLE BOOKS
SAN FRANCISCO

First Chronicle Books LLC paperback edition, published in 2006.

This is a work of fiction. Names, places, characters, and inci-
dents are products of the author's imagination or are used fic-
tionally. Any resemblance to actual people, places, or events is
entirely coincidental.

ISBN-10: 0-8118-5656-9
ISBN-13: 978-0-8118-5656-0

The Library of Congress has cataloged the previous edition
as follows:

Lunstrum, Kirsten Sundberg, 1979-
  This life she's chosen : stories / Kirsten Sundberg Lunstrum.
    p. cm.
  ISBN 0-8118-4513-3
  1. Women—Fiction. I. Title.
  PS3612.U56T48 2004
  813'.6—dc22

                           2004022043

Manufactured in the United States of America

Designed by Brooke Johnson

Distributed in Canada by Raincoast Books
9050 Shaughnessy Street
Vancouver, British Columbia V6P 6E5

10 9 8 7 6 5 4 3 2 1

Chronicle Books LLC
680 Second Street
San Francisco, California 94107

www.chroniclebooks.com

This book is for Nathan.

Acknowledgements

Several people have contributed to the creation of this book. I am indebted to the English Department and the Fiction Writing Program faculty at the University of California, Davis, to the staff at Chronicle Books—particularly Steve Mockus and Calla Devlin—and to my editor, Jay Schaefer, whose kindness and support have been an incredible blessing. I must as well thank Kara Larsen, Phyllis Lunstrum, Jodi Angel, Jennifer Mason, Christien Gholson, Michaela Kahn, Chuck Carlise, Halina Duraj, and Alex Escudé for their continued and valued insight, conversation, support, and friendship. I am most grateful, however, for the uncountable gifts of my husband and family: Nathan Lunstrum, Paul, Dorinda and Britt Sundberg, Marion and Dick Wilkie. Thank you, wholeheartedly and always.

Contents

This Life She's Chosen

Isabelle would arrive in Seattle on the three o'clock flight. She preferred to fly in the afternoon, she'd said on the phone after making the arrangements, as she had never been suited to doing anything in the morning. "I'm too old," she announced. "I've decided to do only what I like now. No more hassles with things like early flights. And anyhow, a person wants a little breakfast before crossing the globe."

"I won't be able to pick you up then," Camille said. She always lied to her mother. "I'm sorry. You'll have to take a cab."

She put the phone down into its cradle and felt only a little guilty. But honestly, she thought, three o'clock, through the heart of traffic.

Only her mother would pick such an hour.

Camille was in the gallery when Isabelle knocked at the front door. The gallery was nothing but a small, dark room with no windows, a billiards table Michael had found at an estate sale, and a new, boxy television set they had bought to replace the older, smaller one. But when she'd looked up these old houses, Camille had found that such rooms were once called galleries, and so she'd begun calling it that to herself, secretly. She liked the elegant sound of it and pictured images of well-dressed couples retiring to galleries for martinis before dinner or coffee after. To Michael, who talked about finding a pinball machine and a dartboard for the space, she obliged and still called it the rec room.

"Mother," Camille said as she opened the heavy front door. She leaned toward Isabelle, waited for her kisses.

"Hello!" Her mother gushed and dropped her bags on the stoop. She raised her hands near her head and fluttered them, as if Camille were something delicious she was about to bite into. Isabelle's gold pendant swung out away from her chest as she inclined her body and pulled Camille into the soft wrinkles of her embrace.

Camille did not put her arms around her mother, but tucked her head into Isabelle's white hair. Isabelle smelled of the metallic, winter air outdoors, and of cigarette smoke, and of the airport and the old leather seats of the cab, entirely unfamiliar.

"Let me take those bags," Camille said, and lifted the straps onto her shoulders, bending her knees with the weight.

Upstairs, Camille showed her mother the guest room. "You're the first to sleep in it," she said, and smiled. She set the luggage down on the floor and straightened, put her hands into the pockets of her gray sweater and looked to her mother.

The room had been done with Camille's friends in mind, women she'd met in college and tried to keep in touch with over the years, women she'd worked with before she married Michael, women who might, she thought, someday come to stay. She'd covered the double bed in a white down comforter, and thrown a red mohair afghan over the foot. It was for winter. In March she would fold it back into the cedar chest and lay out the powder-blue quilt instead. There was an armoire in the corner, as the room did not have a closet, and inside, Camille had hung padded hangers and a lace sachet of lavender she'd found at a store downtown. The window looked out into the bare branches of the backyard oak.

"This will do fine," her mother said. "Should we eat something now? I'm half starved."

Downstairs, the television was still on and Audrey Hepburn was sitting on her catwalk, singing "Moon River." Lately, Camille had taken to watching the afternoon movies, a double feature that ended just before Michael arrived home.

Isabelle settled her plate on her lap and put her feet up on the coffee table. "You're watching trash," she said. "These romances." She shook her head and bit into a square of orange American cheese, the only cheese Camille could find in the refrigerator, though her mother had complained that she should keep looking until she found something better, Brie at least, or Camembert.

"I like romances," Camille said.

"Trash."

Camille uncrossed her legs, stood up, and clicked off the television set.

"A wife always loses her mind," her mother said, picking up her plate as she stood as well. "It's just a question of how long it takes."

Camille was ten when her parents' marriage finally fell apart. Later, when Camille was older, Isabelle confided that she just couldn't do it anymore, it was that simple. When Camille had pressed, wanting a reason, a flaw in the marriage or in her father to blame, Isabelle had laughed at her. "Sometimes, dear, a rose is just a rose." She paused and frowned. "Or something like that. Anyhow, I wanted to leave and we did," she said. "That's all there is."

They'd left her father with the house, the furniture, everything, and took only one suitcase of clothing apiece, nothing else, her mother's rule. Camille tried to bring along the pink spotted umbrella her father had given to her on her last birthday, the Grimm Brothers book he'd read as bedtime stories when she was small, but Isabelle found them in her bag and took them out. "These are wasting space," she said. "Bring things you'll really need." She tossed the umbrella into Camille's closet, chucked the book across the room.

They lived first in an apartment in Chicago, then one in Denver, then in D.C. On weekends, they went to the symphony and the ballet. Isabelle had private French lessons with a tutor and started pronouncing Camille's name with a deep flourish on the second syllable.

In D.C., there had been an Indian restaurant her mother liked just down the street, and on Fridays after school, Camille arrived home to the scent of the curry. Isabelle sat on the floor in her nightgown, the thrift store coffee table she'd bought after the move pushed back and a blanket spread out across the carpet. "Good, yes?" Isabelle always said as they ate. She refused to bring out the forks, and scooped with her fingers at the yellow lump of curry potatoes on her plate. "You couldn't get aloor dum like this in Detroit." She smiled, poked another potato into her mouth.

Camille's father still lived in Detroit. He'd remarried—a mousy, pale-haired woman who had two mousy, pale-haired children of her own. Camille could have gone to stay with them in the summers but never did. Each time she considered the three months away, she imagined her mother eating dinner alone on the front room floor and decided she couldn't go. "I don't want to meet his new family," she told her mother every spring when the invitation came, and Isabelle would pull Camille onto her lap, hold her as if Camille were the one who needed to be looked after.

"That's fine," Isabelle would say, kissing Camille's forehead. "That's just fine, chérie. But you have to be the one to call him. You must be responsible for your decisions."

When she called, her father said only, "I see." And then, "Of course." He sounded far away, unfamiliar. Camille could see him in their old house, his white shirt rolled to the elbows, the undershirt her mother had always complained about just showing at his neck.

Once she'd seen him dance with her mother, around the furniture in the front room, Isabelle in her bare feet at first, coaxing him. He laughed as he stood up. He took Isabelle in his arms and glided her around the room. "Look at your pretty mother," he said to Camille over the music. "Isn't she just too much? She's too much for us."

Into the phone, Camille said, "Maybe next year, though, Dad. Or for the holidays."

Isabelle, who sat listening at the kitchen table, waved her hand to show the phone bill was running up, mouthed the word *good-bye* until Camille said it and hung up the phone.

"Do you miss your father?" Isabelle had asked once, long after they'd left him.

"Yes," Camille nodded. "Every day."

"Oh, darling." Isabelle reached out and touched Camille's hand then, squeezed it. "Stop wasting your childhood."

When Michael arrived home, Isabelle was in the kitchen, a tea towel tied around her waist with a length of packaging twine, and a pot of soup boiling on the stove in front of her. "My daughter can't cook," she said as an introduction. "She doesn't even have an apron."

Michael, his arms still full of his coat and briefcase, turned and looked to Camille where she sat at the kitchen table, as if unsure about whether he should defend her or make fast friends with her mother. Camille shrugged.

"I would apologize to you for not raising her better if you were anyone but her husband," Isabelle said, and laughed at her own joke. She had pulled her white hair back into a loose knot to cook, and under the warm lights of their kitchen, in the glow from the hanging rack of silver and copper-bottomed pans near the stove, she looked jovial, festive, benign.

"She cooks," Michael began, then paused. Camille waited to see how he would finish his sentence. *Beautifully*, she thought for him. *Deliciously. Like a pro.* But he left it at that, stooped to kiss Camille's forehead, and disappeared upstairs to change his clothes.

Later, in bed and in the blue darkness of their room, Camille rolled over, searching for his body beneath the weight of sheets and blankets. "She won't be here forever," she said. "Two weeks and then she'll go." She pressed her face into the bend at the back of his neck.

"I don't mind her." He was tired, his voice halfway into sleep already.

Camille listened to his breath, to the wind rattling the old casement windows and the ticks of rain against their purpled, wavy glass.

"I like her," he said. He sighed and shifted. "You'll tell her to stop calling me Mee-shell, though?" His hand found her thigh, and he squeezed it, rolled away from her to sleep.

Camille lay looking up at the ceiling, her arms folded on top of her chest. She counted back over the dinners she'd made Michael in the last week: pot roast and potatoes; meat loaf and green salad; a turkey-carrot potpie. All sturdy, solid foods, she thought, none necessarily requiring an apron. She let out the breath she hadn't realized she'd been holding and turned onto her side, closed her eyes, and waited for sleep.

Once Camille left for college, her mother left the country. "We're French," she had told Camille over the phone. "Or our family is. It's just taken me this long to come home."

Camille did not argue. She didn't remind her mother that she'd been born in Detroit. That the family name had been pronounced *Du-boys* for several generations.

Isabelle began peppering her letters with French words and phrases Camille couldn't always translate but generally understood. *Mon beau rêve is going well*, she wrote. She began addressing them to *Ma Petite Ancre*, nothing but a little joke, she said, but Camille didn't find it funny. Once Camille married Michael, the joke changed, and above her new street address her mother wrote *La Petite Femme* in loopy, feminine cursive.

Isabelle had not come to their wedding, though Camille had folded a small note into one of the blue invitations, asking her directly to attend.

Mother, she wrote. *I would like to see your face on my wedding day. Please come. ~ Camille*

Fille, her mother responded. *Here you are. I wish you luck, at best. ~ Isabelle*

Inside the envelope, Camille found a smiling Polaroid image of her mother's face.

Then Isabelle moved to Marseilles and took a job as cook at a convent. "The nuns don't mind me," she assured Camille over the phone.

Camille winced whenever she thought about her mother in a convent. It brought to her mind scenes from *Babette's Feast*, an embarrassing image of her mother stirring up passions, so to speak, and believing in a silly, Hollywood way that her food would move the nuns to lust or grief or joy. She wondered if her mother even saw the romantic façade she'd put up as her life.

"It doesn't matter that I'm not Catholic," Isabelle had said, "as long as I'm quiet, and I keep cooking for them."

Camille could not imagine her mother ever being quiet.

When Camille made her way downstairs in the morning, she found her mother already awake and dressed and sitting at the kitchen table with the newspaper spread in front of her. Sarah Vaughan was on the speakers in the other room, and there was a French press Camille had never seen before on the counter, full of coffee.

"I brought my own press," her mother said. She looked up at Camille from the news, smiled. She had stopped wearing any makeup years before, and Camille had remembered her as pale, her skin waxy and tight, as if she'd wanted it all—France and the rest of it—just a little too much. But her face had softened, the skin slacked a bit around her eyes and at her jaw line, and the color was high in her cheeks again. Maybe it was age, Camille thought. Or the good influence of nuns. She smiled to herself, poured a cup of coffee, and sat down at the table across from her mother.

Isabelle folded the paper and laid her hands neatly on top of it. She beamed. "You like your coffee? You should have it with milk, easier on the stomach, less American. You've all phased out the taste bud in this country." She stood up, went to the refrigerator, and pulled out a tray of sliced fruit—red gala apples, bright wedges of orange. And from the oven, a loaf of sweet bread, warm and wrapped in towels.

"You baked?" Camille asked. "I didn't smell it."

"You've gotten into the habit of sleeping in. Your husband left hours ago, months." Isabelle cut thick servings of the bread and laid them on two plates that she carried to the table.

"Listen," she said. "I was thinking about all this," she waved her hand at the house around her, a big sweep, "about you and Michael, and I thought the least you deserve is a party." Isabelle pursed her lips and decided on three apple slices, nudged them onto her plate with her finger. "I would like to have a party, here," she went on. "I'll cook." She crossed her arms over her wide chest, raised her eyebrows, and smiled. "Oui?" Isabelle nodded as if it had been decided. "Oui." She picked up her fork, plunged its tines into an apple.

It seemed, a few days later as they arrived at the grocery store, that the party had been in Isabelle's mind all along. She pulled a list from the bulge of her purse as Camille wheeled a cart through the bins of produce. Camille had been to this store only once, with Michael, to buy a bottle of wine on their way to an office party his manager at the bank had held.

"I need endive," her mother announced, "and Jerusalem artichokes, shallots and garlic and herbes de Provence, if you think we can find that in this country." She snorted slightly, smoothed her list between her thick fingers.

When she was young, none of the other girls from school had ever wanted to eat at Camille's. They would come for a slumber party, because her mother would give them the front room to sleep in, would dance with them to her jazz albums, and let them stand on the back stoop in nothing but their babydolls, smoking her skinny cigarettes. But they always went out for pizza before coming over or shakes at the drive-in downtown. Isabelle might serve anything, they said, and wrinkled their noses. She might serve melon soup. She might serve chicken liver pâté.

Camille had offered no defense for her mother. Everything they said was true, and she could forgive them for not wanting to come. *My mother,* she'd say, and roll her eyes. She always felt sick saying it, though, wrenched in her middle. And when she got home to Isabelle, she would eat a little more of the food her friends couldn't stand, to make up for their absence, and for what she'd said.

"Jerusalem artichokes," her mother was going on now, "were sent to France by Champlain after he tasted one in Canada." She smiled at Camille, tossed two heads of red-leaf lettuce into their cart. "You didn't know that, did you? It's true, though. I read it somewhere."

Standing beside her mother, Camille was aware of herself in a way that she had not been in a long time. She felt her mother in the way she walked, in the way she moved her arms and held her shoulders tightly back, her head erect. She wondered if strangers passing them could see the resemblance. If they looked at her mother's high forehead and then at hers, at her mother's height, her square, masculine shoulders and broad bottom, and saw how Camille's body was, though twenty-five years younger and somewhat slimmer, the same.

Her mother had thrown a burgundy fringed silk wrap around her shoulders before leaving the house, and she shifted it now as she walked beside Camille. It hung down below the small of her back, and its fabric moved as she moved, billowed out at her elbows and fell into a neat drape around her frame when she stopped to bend over the open containers of kalamata and cerignola olives. Her pearl-drop earrings swung at her earlobes, and her hair was the fine, flat white of bone china under the poor fluorescent lighting in the store. "Yum," her mother cooed, holding out a purpled olive. "Yum-yum, dear. Taste this." Isabelle licked her fingers, made little, sucking smacks with her lips.

"No, thank you," Camille said, and pushed the cart away from Isabelle.

At home, settled on the couch, Camille folded herself into an afghan and watched Gene Kelly and Danny Kaye dance across the television screen. This week was musicals. Later today, *Singin' in the Rain*, and tomorrow afternoon, *South Pacific*. Maybe she would make her mother sit down with her, watch silently as the little white children learned to sing in patois.

She could hear her mother upstairs, riffling through cookbooks in the kitchen, sorting through the few recipes Camille had decided to clip from women's magazines and save. She could hear her mother's shuffled footsteps on the hardwood floor, the clanging of pots and pans, and the ceramic rattle of plates being taken from and then re-stacked in the cupboard.

"Let me give you this," her mother had said as they'd left the grocery store. "Let me give you one night of your life when you can just be a guest in your home."

"Mother," Camille drew in a narrow, exasperated breath. "I love my husband."

"Of course you do," Isabelle sighed. "But none of this has to do with him." She took the cart from Camille and moved ahead between the racks of bread and rolls, the silk of her wrap dancing freely around her waist as she went.

When she met him, Michael seemed familiar to Camille in a way she could not explain. He was slight and fair, blue eyed. He did not ever raise his voice. He smelled of the wool sweaters he wore over his dress shirts to combat the wet, Seattle cold, and of the medicinal lozenges he kept in his bedside drawer, and of milky Ivory soap.

None of these traits were what she had first recognized in him, though. No, it was something else, something she could not name, and Camille found herself looking for it all the time. Waiting for it to present itself to her, the way a road sign, though stationary and always standing in the blurry periphery of one's vision, suddenly jumps out into the roadway to yell *Stop*.

The afternoon of the party, Isabelle banished Camille to her bedroom. "I need room," Isabelle said. Her face flamed from the heat of the kitchen, where the oven had been going all morning, and from her excitement.

In her bedroom upstairs, Camille lay back on the bed and opened up a magazine. She flipped to a dog-earred page, with glossy images of movie actresses, statuesque and glimmering in sequined gowns and thin-strapped sandals. They seemed to her Venuses, sprung from nothing, suddenly, to be photographed and admired. She could not imagine the mother of a single one of them, the ancient, less beautiful versions of themselves, the hags and the widows and the dying. The entirely unglamorous generation that had birthed these girls. She couldn't see it, and for a moment, she felt the pinch of jealousy for them. They were not daughters. *And they are definitely not wives,* her mother would say.

She closed the magazine, tucked it beneath the bed, and got up to dress for the party.

As she descended the staircase, Camille caught the scents of garlic and cayenne. Michael was at the stereo, adjusting the sound on the same Sarah Vaughan album as the other morning, though this time Sarah's voice seemed deeper, and glinted, as if the sound had been edged in tinsel wrapping and was catching light.

"Lovely," he said when he saw her.

Camille had put on a suit: an ivory laced camisole beneath a jacket and long, creased pants. She'd washed her hair and clipped it back at the nape of her neck with a pearled clasp. "I'd hoped the weather would clear," she said. From where she stood at the mid-point of the stairway, she could see through the fanlight above the front door. The sky was just beginning to darken, and the afternoon clouds had not lifted.

She moved down the stairs and opened the door and stepped outside. The points of her heels dug into the lines of mud between the stones of the walk, and she gently tugged to free them. Michael turned on the outdoor lights, and they beamed small circles onto the wet grass of the lawn, lit the path toward the house just enough in the dusky dark for Camille to see a few steps ahead of herself. She went to the mailbox and turned back to look at the house. It was angular and imposing, large for just the two of them. *Embarrassingly large,* her mother had said, but still not enough. Isabelle had said it was pretentious, with its stone cornices above each of the lower-story windows and the front door, its mahogany moldings inside, and the wisteria-covered pergola out back.

Who are you to talk about pretensions? Camille had wanted to yell. She liked the house. She liked the way it looked like the kind of place she would want to live in, neat and polished and traditional. She liked the brass doorknocker, the gleaming planks of the wood floors, and the boxy row of hedges that fenced the front yard from the sidewalk and the street. Inside, the house was uncluttered. Michael's white shirts were pressed and hung in his closet. Her cuffed trousers had been folded on their seams and placed into the dresser drawers. The mat in the guest bathroom was clean, and the dust had been swept from beneath the bookshelves in the front room. She liked the solid dove brown of the house's exterior, and the way it sat square on its plot of property, last on the street, so that each time she turned the corner and saw it, the house was there, expected, a certain stop to the road.

She tried to look up at the house now as the guests would in a few moments, its dark hulk against the gray sky, the rain-logged and dripping leaves that still remained on the plum tree near the front door.

It had been Michael's house before he met her. "I know you'll love it," he said when they began dating.

And she always had.

Isabelle emerged from the kitchen with the sound of the first guests arriving. She was wearing a red sheer blouse over a red camisole and a string of shining, colored-glass beads. She'd pinned her hair up, letting long wisps of it fall down at her neck and her temples, where they were already curling with her sweat and the heat of the kitchen. She stood at Michael and Camille's side, shaking hands and being introduced.

"Isabelle," Camille said, "this is Darius and Imogen Smitt. Darius works with Michael at the bank." She smiled, stepped back to let the Smitts shake her mother's hand.

Behind them, Camille introduced the other guests as they appeared at the front door. "Mark and Bill are on Michael's team at the bank," she heard herself say. "Susan is his assistant. Christine is a manager in another department." Camille touched her palm to her mother's back, watched Isabelle take each guest's hand into her own two and pump it, grinning, glossy and pink-faced with the evening.

There were hors d'oeuvres on the coffee table, canapés and crackers, and a salmon mousse for dipping. Michael moved between the kitchen and the front room, stopping at each circle of conversation to pass out glasses of scotch and wine. Camille had met all of these people at Michael's office parties—she had been to their homes—but their faces all looked too alike somehow now, wide and scrubbed and blank, but smiling. They had all come in suits, directly from work, the women in suits too, similar to her own. Blue or black or beige trousers and matching jackets. Seed pearls around every neck.

Camille made her way between them, catching snipped fragments of bank conversation, end-of-the-workday talk. Whenever she joined a group, however, the topic shifted to their families or the movie they'd seen last Saturday, and eventually she was left alone while people went to find the powder room or searched out Michael for another drink.

Isabelle caught her at one point and leaned in close, whispered, "Are any of these people *your* friends?"

Camille raised a finger to her ear, tapped it as if the room had become too loud to hear the question. She excused herself then, and slipped away into the kitchen.

On the tabletop her mother had spread all of the dishes she'd prepared. A pot of mussel stew, baked salmon with Pernod, a large wooden bowl of salad. Camille bent and breathed in the smell of anise, of onions and butter. There were trays of cheeses and crusted bread rounds. A platter of red and green grapes, and another on which her mother had drizzled chocolate and raspberry sauces around a smooth, chocolate gâteau. Isabelle had placed a stack of glass dishes on the table, had polished and lined up the rows of silver spoons and forks and knives, the folded white napkins. There were extra wineglasses and several opened and unopened bottles of wine and scotch and whiskey, and on the counter, coffee cups and saucers waiting for later in the evening.

These were her dishes, things she had been given by Michael's friends and parents, by people she had known, when she and Michael had married. There were the silver serving spoon and fork with the decorative handles; her silver candlestick holders on the table, and in them, a flickering set of ivory tapers she remembered buying herself, last Christmas. There was the wreath of dried eucalyptus and cranberries on the wall above the stove; the linen tablecloth; the braided red rug. Camille felt weighted by these things as she looked at them, by the heavy, orange light put off by the candles in the dark kitchen. Beyond the door she could hear the low plodding of the music, the thudding of dress shoes and the horse-hoof staccato of high heels as people began dancing.

Camille pushed herself toward the doorway and stood a moment there, her hand flat on the door, then shoved out into the light of the front room. Her mother had set votives along the top of the mantel, and their flames jumped and reflected in quick, bright flashes in the wide mirror above it. The song had changed, and this one was upbeat, Sarah's voice a flutter in her throat, the next note unpredictable. In the middle of the floor, couples danced. The women had abandoned their jackets to the couch, and the men had loosed their ties, so that the low knots swung as they twirled their wives.

Mark Thorgerson had Isabelle in his arms in the center of the room, and she was a swirl of red where he spun her. She had shaken out her hairpins, or they had simply fallen, and her hair hung down to the middle of her back. She looked light, Camille thought, the way Gene Kelly or Vera-Ellen seemed light when they danced, as if joy had somehow lifted their feet from the ground.

Camille felt Michael's hand at her waist and turned, rested her head on his shoulder. She felt too heavy to go on standing. She put her arm around him, held to his belt with her fingers.

"Your mother's the one who started the dancing," he said. He looked between her and her mother, paused for a moment, then chuckled. "She's too much," he said, "dancing with Mark." Michael rubbed his palm against the small of her back and leaned forward to kiss her cheek.

Camille slipped her arm from his embrace and crossed the room to sit on the couch beside the heap of crumpled jackets, the scarves and wrinkled neckties that had been dropped there. She could see her mother from where she sat, her mother's flushed face, and the deep lines around her mouth as Isabelle laughed and said something to her new dance partner.

In the blurry periphery of her vision, she could see Michael as well, still standing where she'd left him, his hands shoved down into his pockets, his back straight and pressed against the frame of the door.

Camille settled back against the couch and waited for her heart, which had quickened, to slow again.

She watched her mother dance.

The Skin of My Fingers

Our first night at the hospital a mother came in delivering breech. Her water had broken early in the day, and she'd been laboring for hours. She could not have been much older than I was then (maybe younger, even—nineteen or twenty), and she had the round, fleshy face of a child still, her eyes puffed and squeezed to slits, and weepy with exhaustion. The girl's gown was pulled up so that the mound of her belly showed, the skin there yellowed and zippered in stretch marks, which were puckered and shiny, like snags in satin fabric. I stepped away from her, and Amanda caught me by the arm. "Look at that color," she whispered. "I bet no oxygen. He'll come out crippled." She squeezed my wrist in the circle of her long fingers. "Or dead."

The delivery room already smelled of blood, warm and uncomfortably familiar and earthy as black dirt. The nurse in charge, a slight, sharp-faced woman with a shrill voice, handed me a paper cup of ice chips. "Feed these to her," she directed, and I moved around the bed, gripping the metal rail, the disintegrating cup. Now and then, as I slipped ice into the girl's mouth, my fingers touched her lips, which were wet with the ice and her saliva. She licked them then, impatient with my fussing, and I felt the cold tip of her tongue glide across my fingernails and over the skin of my fingers, before I took my hand back, wiped it across the fabric of my pants.

This was my first delivery. I had seen puppies delivered, in a cardboard box behind my mother's clothes dryer at home, though it seemed their birth was so much faster than this, easier, that each time I turned my head away for a moment another puppy slithered out, and I had missed everything. This delivery was slow and hard. Several times I left the room to get more ice just so that I could leave, pause in the hallway with its cleaner scents of rubbing alcohol and disinfectant. The doctor stepped out at one point and found me bent over just outside the door, my face down near my knees where it seemed I could breathe without feeling the knot of a gag rise in my throat. "Get up, Louise," he said, stern. "This is nothing. They'll both be fine."

Amanda was not so new to birth. We'd come to Juneau together, from eastern Washington, to finish out our training as nurses. The hospital at home in Omak was small and already fully staffed, so they spread our class out, shipping us like mail-order brides to towns we had never heard of in Nevada and Idaho, Oregon and Alaska, where we worked swing shifts and night shifts and cleaned more dirty bedpans than any of us could have predicted.

Amanda said she'd seen plenty of births before on her parents' farm, and, she assured me, working labor and delivery, though it was not her chosen field either, would not be the shock to her system that it would be to mine. "There's more mess than you'd think," she'd said our first night in Juneau, as if to warn me. She spoke always like an older sister, and now and then laid her hand on my arm, if what she was going to say seemed to her too graphic for my imagination. "They come out covered in a coating of ricotta cheese."

"Vernix," I corrected. I was a good student and liked the textbook descriptions of birth if not the real thing. I had written out the scientific terms on index cards to memorize and liked their clean, black-ink order, their lettered management of the body.

"Right," Amanda said. "They come out covered in vernix. And mucus and amniotic water and blood."

She knew this all from textbooks too. Her experience was only with animal deliveries, cows and sheep and kittens. She said she'd missed half her classes every spring when the cows were calving. We sat together on the beach our first night in Juneau, a blanket wrapped around our shoulders because we weren't yet adjusted to the temperature, and she told me about her family's farm. It was in Riverside, up the hill from Omak and across the river, which is why we hadn't gone to high school together, nor even met until beginning nurses training a few months before.

"They'd eat their placentas," she said about the sheep. "But if there were twins, my dad would only let the ewe eat one and he'd bury the other. My mom said the placenta was good for the soil. She had him bury it in the front yard and marked the spot with a Popsicle stick so she could plant roses there the next year. Those roses kept better color. Or so she said, anyway."

Amanda sat with her back to mine as she talked, to trap as much heat between us as we could. I could not see her, sitting that way, but I could picture her face as I listened, broad and flat as her name, with her blunt-cut farmer's daughter bangs and the smattering of freckles across her nose that she tried to cover with pancake makeup and powder too pale for her pink skin.

"I killed a calf one year," she said. "I was just a kid when it happened. I didn't know any better." She shifted on the wet sand. The cold was already seeping up through the seats of our jeans, the fog that hung over Gastineau Channel spreading out, creeping up the beach and blurring the lights of the city on the other side of the water. Fog on the island was like a live thing, rising and arching, then settling out to a flat, thick white, lying still on the black surface of the channel.

"I thought I'd feed it like my father did every morning," Amanda said. "I'd watched him before, mixing the feed with a little hose water in the trough. Only I couldn't read yet and I got the wrong bag." She snuffed a laugh. "I mixed the calf some cement and the dummy ate it. That shows you how stupid cows are. His stomach bloated, and then the cement got hard in there like a big rock. He couldn't process it. My father couldn't lift him with all that cement to haul too, so he ended up just dragging the calf by his back legs out of the barn. This was early spring, so Dad just left him there a few weeks until the ground thawed. Then he could bury him."

Amanda stopped, and I could feel the movement of her rib cage against my back as she breathed.

"The mother cow bellowed the whole time. She wouldn't lick my hand anymore when I fed her after that either. I think she knew."

Later, I watched the breech baby's delivery. He came out with the cord wrapped twice around his neck, his face fat and glistening, blue as a new bruise, his nostrils and mouth thick with plugs of mucus and vernix that the nurse in charge sucked out with a bulb syringe. His body was slick with his mother's blood.

He lived, though. So did his mother.

Amanda and I shared rent on a house on Douglas Island, across the channel from the hospital. We weren't particularly close friends, but there was the obligation of staying together because we had come from the same place. The house we leased had been white at one point, but it had faded to gray by the time we moved in. The siding was bubbled from years of absorbing rainwater and slimy with the same sheen of algae that skimmed all of the sidewalks in town and the white, cinder-block sides of the hospital. Everything in Juneau seemed to be slowly taking on the color and body of the island itself, the wood of the buildings softening to sponge, the aluminum roofs greening the same shade as the Sitka spruce and seaweed.

Our house was situated at the top of a steep hill that we were afraid to drive the car up or down. The car had come with the house and was a breaking-down old Dodge. I tried to tell the landlord we wouldn't need the car, that we didn't want to be responsible for it falling into further disrepair, but he laughed. "Cheaper to give it to you than to have it barged off the island to a junk heap down south," he said. "Everything goes at some point. Drive it till it dies, then just leave it."

He was right, of course; everywhere I looked in town later I noticed old cars, long past their prime, parked along the sides of streets, and two or three shells on the back lawn of nearly every house, along with molding sofas and unwanted bed frames and other unfamiliar trash. The beach was littered too, with metal odds and ends left over from the mines that had closed midcentury. Lengths of pipe and metal rings and sometimes bigger pieces of metal I couldn't make up a use for, all of them thick with a buildup of rust that bled out, oranging a sort of aura in the sand, just let go of, abandoned.

The Dodge did run, though its motor had a burbled, water-logged sound that kept us from ever driving farther than the hospital or the grocery store. We parked at the bottom of the hill after work every night and walked the rest of the way up to the house, puffing halos of our own breath and listening to the smack-ing sound of our thick-soled hospital shoes on the wet pavement as we climbed. Sometimes we sang songs we remembered from grade school or from home: "Roll On, Columbia, Roll On," or the whiny and ancient Patsy Cline songs both our mothers loved to play.

"Do you miss it much?" Amanda asked me once.

"Home, you mean?"

"I don't mean your house exactly," she said, "but the place. Not your family either. Of course you miss them," she winked at me. Amanda had made a list the first day we arrived of all the things she would do now that she was not in Riverside. She would drink a glass of Carlo Rossi every night with dinner; she would wear the red lipstick her mother thought looked cheap on her complex-ion; and on Sundays she would skip Mass and never get out of bed before eleven.

"No," I said. "I'm not homesick. Not at all."

Nearly every week a letter came from my mother. *Hey to you in the North!* she began, as if I'd been marooned in the Arctic Circle. *All's well down here. Weather cloudy on Tuesday, and smell of snow in the air. Saw Canada Geese flying South this morning, and last of the leaves fallen in yard. Apple tree is bare again—Dad will cut down next weekend. That's about it from this end of the world. Had thought I'd see more letters, but assume you're up to your neck in busy. Love from everyone, Your Mother*

At seven, when I took my lunch break at the hospital each night, I thought of her and my father and sister in the square, saltbox house I'd grown up in. I could guess exactly where they were and what they were doing, and I pictured them sometimes as I ate my cheese sandwich and peeled the little Satsuma oranges I'd gotten used to eating as a workday treat. My father would be reading, and my sister doing homework in the bedroom we'd shared upstairs, but my mother would still be in the kitchen. I saw her bent over the dishwasher, finding a spot for the last plate, moving to the sink to fill the kettle for tea, scraping the last bites of food from the pans into the trash bag. I felt nostalgic for them in those moments, in the lunchroom with its sterile cafeteria chairs and table always dusted with crumbs, sticky from somebody else's meal. The hospital piped wordless, fuzzy versions of popular songs into the room and kept the heat down low so that I had to huddle into myself as I ate.

The house wasn't as I remembered it, though. That summer, before I left, my mother renovated it. She bought aluminum siding, to keep the weather out, she said, and had new, white cupboards installed in the kitchen, new, real tiles laid where before there had been orange-red linoleum, patterned to look like brick. Over the kitchen sink, a square panel of wallboard was knocked out to make room for a garden window, where my mother had in mind glazed pots of oregano and rosemary and mint. She would be able to look out and see the hills across town from that window while she peeled potatoes or washed lettuce in the evenings, and in the morning, the sun coming up over the bare, brown rise of Omak Mountain, the same mountain she'd been waking up to her entire life, through a brand new window.

"What do you think?" she had asked, standing beside me in the new kitchen.

"It's not like home now," I said. "I don't like it."

My mother folded her arms across her chest and turned away from me. "You're leaving, Louise. You won't have to dislike it much longer."

In Juneau, I imagined my mother doing the dishes in front of her garden window in the house that was no longer mine, and I felt a lonely, desperate kind of freedom.

Amanda and I had neighbors up on the top of the hill. To our left a narrow red house stood on stilts, precarious and quaint. There was a porch on the street-facing side of the house that seemed stuck on only to balance out and steady the structure, to keep it from sliding right down the slippery hill and into the channel. The man who lived there—Mr. Forrel—often came out to his porch to smoke, wearing only his plaid bathrobe and his baseball cap, mesh with a green bill. It was the kind of hat our fathers and uncles wore at home, and it meant to us work and tractors and the dark, oily smell those men always had.

Mr. Forrel lived alone, though now and then we'd see an unfamiliar car in the drive, a little blue hatchback sometimes, and other times a brown coupe or a gray sedan. We decided they belonged to his female friends, and we giggled when we heard them start up and drive off after only fifteen minutes or a half hour. "He's quick," Amanda would say, which was my cue to say, "as a one-eyed eel," and then we would laugh. He was a fisherman, and beneath the porch he'd stacked round, metal nets and beside them a pile of fat, white raindrop-shaped buoys. Each time I passed the house I thought of breasts (because of the buoys and the women) and of the dead and curling bodies of salmon (because of the nets and the stink that rose from them).

To the right, and set back in a thick stand of spruce, was the Vagens' house, the only other house on our hill. It was small but tidy, and unpainted, so that the red-toned wood of its siding had a raw and unfinished look. A neat wall of cut wood for burning rested against one side of the house, and when Amanda and I reached the top of the hill each night at eleven, a clean, blue line of smoke was always drifting up from the stovepipe through the bluer branches of the spruce trees.

"They're lowlifes," Amanda said, looking at the house in the trees as we stood on our own front porch, stripping off wet layers of clothes before going inside for the night. It was raining, and the walk up the hill had soaked the white legs of our uniform pants, drenched our bare heads. It was cold enough to see our breath again, but not cold enough to snow.

"You don't even know them," I said.

"I can tell. They've got that woodpile, instead of electrical or gas heat. He probably doesn't work. He's probably on disability or unemployment." She leaned over and shook her wet hair near me like a dog would do, until I swatted at her with my scarf. "There are probably six snotty-nosed babies in that house right now as we speak," she said.

I winced when she said things like that. She'd done the same at work, watching the other nurses and the doctors until she felt she had figured them out. Her assessments weren't always flattering, but once she'd assigned someone her judgment, he was familiar to her, and Amanda would be friendly the next time they met. I understood the habit because it was home. My mother had told me once that she'd had a friend in Riverside whose family kept nineteen cats. The cats were all skinny and losing fur in places, and would reach out from beneath a chair to scratch any ankle that passed them. It made her believe that all of Riverside was infested with such animals, diseased dogs and unkempt horses and ignorant, ill-mannered people. Knowing this sort of trashiness was rooted in every Riverside resident, my mother could adjust her own manners when she met one of them. Mrs. Routhe from the church and Anna Lipton at the IGA were both from that side of the hill, and my mother spoke to them always with a sugared, gushing kindness that she believed was generous. Behind it was the house of cats, though, and the same clumsy, small-town manners she couldn't see in herself. She always finished the story by saying, "That house just reeked of cat piss."

Nights in Alaska were darker than any night I'd seen at home, and more silent. In January the sun had begun to go down around two or three o'clock and didn't rise until nine the next morning. All those hours the darkness kept thickening, getting deeper and spreading itself across the expanse of the sky. On the rare clear nights, I liked looking up past the tops of the spruce to the milk-swirls of stars. I always expected to feel my solitude then, but what I felt instead was something more adolescent and self-centered, the muddle of my own confusions reflected back to me.

Most nights, after work, I liked to sit on the porch alone, bundled into the winter jacket I had bought with my own saved money just before leaving home, the blanket from my bed wrapped around my pajamas at the waist. I couldn't always sleep well right away with the white fluorescence of the hospital lights still bright behind my eyes, and my back smarting when I tried to lie down because I'd been on my feet all day. When I could fall asleep, I often dreamed about the hospital, changing bedding and stitching episiotomies in my sleep, so that in the morning it felt as if I'd worked a double shift instead of getting any rest at all.

"You see that?" a voice said from the street one night.

I walked out to the railing of the porch. "I'm sorry?"

"Orion there," Mr. Vagen said, and I could see his gloved hand pointing up. "He's the hunter. And over there, the dippers." He walked farther out into the street from his drive but kept his voice low, so that I had to keep moving closer, off the porch and onto the street as well, to hear him. He wore yellow leather gloves and a down jacket that filled out his figure, made him look like a large man from where I'd been standing on the porch, but when I walked toward him, I saw that he was thin and tall and carrying a load of wood in his arms. "I was just looking at the stars," he said, "and I saw you over there doing the same."

"No," I said. "I don't know the constellations."

"Well," he said. He bent and laid his wood down in the street, then stood up to point again. "Orion, with the three-star belt and the rest of them hanging down there like a dagger. Story goes he was blinded. Some say for an indiscretion I won't mention now, but basically, he couldn't stay at home. He was blinded, and he had to go out searching for his sight. Only after a long journey could he see again."

"And then?" I asked. I wanted to know about the end of the story. Once the hunter had his sight back, did he go home again then?

But Mr. Vagen took a breath and went on. "Follow Orion over, you can just see the panhandle of the Big Dipper." He kept his hand up. "Follow the line of your arm," he said. I could smell the wood on him, and the warm scent of his body inside his coat when he leaned toward me to lift my arm and direct my own finger to the right position.

"Okay," I said. "I see it." I didn't; I saw clusters of stars and the blank spaces between them, but when I said it he stepped back, bent down again to gather up the wood.

"I never see a bear," he said. "Just a ladle. Simple I guess."

I wasn't sure what he meant by that, *simple*. The seeing, or him?

"You're the new nurses, I suppose? Babies, I heard." He looked at me, and I nodded. "My wife's expecting," he said. I meant to congratulate him, but he picked up the last log and began to cross the street toward his house.

In the middle of the road he stopped and turned back toward me. "You know, she can't see them either," he said. "My wife. She says it looks like diamonds, or ice crystals let go." He smiled. Behind him, smoke was already rising from the chimney of his house. "Anyway," he said. He raised his hand to say good night and disappeared up his driveway.

My mother continued to send a letter every week, each of them written out longhand instead of typed, my name and the date in capital letters at the top of the page. *LOUISE*, she wrote. *Hope hospital is treating you good up there. Everybody here is so proud. Told Mrs. Ringheim you were in AK and she could hardly believe it. (She remembered that time you ran away from home—found you under the forsythia bush.) Wants me to ask if your igloo stays warm enough! Dad took down Christmas lights (finally!). House looks naked now (maybe I can find some Easter lights? Ha!) Love from everyone, Your Mother*

I opened her letters outside and read them standing in front of the mailbox, then dropped them into the trash before going in the house. I knew, though she would never say it, that my mother was saving my letters, that she was keeping them where she kept every letter and card she received, in the shoe box on the desk, beside the juice can full of pens, and I felt both guilty and pleased with myself for throwing hers away.

"I'm expecting you to write," she'd said on the day I left for Juneau. "I'll write to you too." She smiled and reached to squeeze my hand in hers.

She had driven me to Spokane herself, because my father had to work. We left early so that we could have lunch at the Queen Mary Hotel downtown before my flight. The restaurant was on the first floor of the hotel, which was a large, stone, turn-of-the-century building with heavy wooden doors and red carpets and windows with the kind of thick glass that made me think I was looking out from the inside of a Mason jar. I hadn't ever thought about my mother knowing of places like this and wondered how it was that she did—if some boyfriend before my father had brought her to the restaurant on a date, or if she had made a trip to Spokane by herself maybe, in that time I usually forgot to consider, when she still thought about getting out of Omak, when she was still just Marie and not yet my mother.

She ordered for us both, unfolding her white napkin into her lap, holding up her glass for the waitress to fill with water.

"Your father would want a hamburger," she said. "Then he'd complain that we could get the same thing for a dollar at the drive-through down the street." She smiled, sipped her water, and folded her hands in her lap.

It had begun to snow outside as we'd driven in, big, airy flakes that drifted down and melted on the pavement. My back was to the window, but there was a round, old-fashioned mirror on the wall across the dining room, and I could see the reflection of us in it: the neat gray curls of my mother's head, and my own small, plain face; the window behind me with its lace curtains, and the snow still falling outside.

"You don't think this will stop the flight, do you?" I asked.

"No, of course not," my mother said. "We'd just get a room if it did, and you'd be on the plane tomorrow."

I felt a knot I hadn't realized was there untie itself in my stomach at the idea of being snowed in, checking into a motel with my mother, not getting on the plane. "We could sleep at a motel near the airport," I said, "so we wouldn't have to drive so far in the morning."

"Well, yes, by the airport. I'm going home today, though," my mother said. "I meant we'd get a room for you." She leaned forward to squeeze my hand again. "Louise," she said. "This was your choice."

Later, at the airport, she dropped me at the curb. "I don't want to pay for parking," she said. "Not for just a few minutes. Anyway, I should hit the road before it gets dark. Your father'll worry if I'm too late." She waited in the car while I unloaded my bags from the trunk, then left the motor running and got out to say good-bye and hug me. I knew I would be able to smell her on my coat for the rest of the day, the Avon perfume she'd been wearing since high school, the garlic and onion and garden dirt scent that was part of her skin.

I had expected her to cry once we reached the airport, to make the kind of scene I would be embarrassed by, but wanted. She didn't. She got back in the car and pulled away. I heard her honk from the corner as I made my way inside.

That night, opening my suitcase in Juneau, I found she had tucked her first letter to me inside, the paper unfolded on top of my clothes, wrinkled from the trip.

LOUISE,

Can't believe you're already gone. Seems like last night you were born, and me thinking you were my girl . . . Dad says we'll come up this summer, but you know how it is. This is just how things go, though—we let go. You'll live. So will I.

The next paragraph was about the weather, the afghan she was knitting for the couch, the new recipe she wanted to try for Sunday dinner.

I sat on my new bed, my suitcase at my feet and the deep Juneau darkness wide beyond the bedroom window at my back. I read and reread my mother's letter, then got up and wadded it into a ball. It was the first letter I threw into the trash.

The storm that had been predicted for weeks finally arrived at the end of the month, and Juneau was buried in snow. The hospital was busy, so I moved to the emergency room for a double shift, to help sew stitches and take temperatures and worry about the frostbitten fingertips and noses of fishermen. It was noisy there, with children crying, and people carrying on conversations, and the constant mechanical sound of the elevator doors. The air smelled of bodies and wet hair and urine. Amanda had been assigned a shift there too, and as I moved from one patient to the next I looked to spot her in the crowd. I felt easier when I could find her, as if the room still had a familiar center and I had not been lost.

"I was thinking of home," she said that evening. Her shift was over, though I was just on a break between my two, and we'd gone upstairs to our unit to eat lunch. "I put a toe back on today," she said. "Cut off with an axe—through a boot." She was impressed. "I remembered your story about Mr. Pederson and the ice saw." Amanda stood up and threw her paper bag into the trash, smiled. "You can take the girl out of the country. Isn't that what people say?" She laughed at herself and waved from the door as she left.

The second shift seemed long without her there, and I counted twenty hours since I had last slept by the time I could go for the night. I gathered my coat and purse and made it nearly out the door before seeing Mr. Vagen standing at the admitting desk in his down coat, his hands in the yellow gloves he wore to haul wood. At his side, his wife sat in a wheelchair, wearing a red bathrobe and a plastic hospital bracelet.

I kept on toward the door. I had the feeling of seeing what I should not have, of being caught spying, and I fingered the bus token in my pocket. But he looked up from his wife.

"I saw the other girl leave already," he said. "We've been here that long."

Mrs. Vagen turned to me then, as if I could persuade the nurse at the desk to let them go, never mind the paperwork. But when I didn't move, she closed her eyes and ignored me. She had graying blond hair held back in a messy braid, and a narrow face that seemed mostly gray too, but not old, not wrinkled, just softened to the dull, flat color of clay.

"If you're needing a ride back," Mr. Vagen said, "you can come with us. It'll be a minute."

I couldn't see how I could say no once he'd offered, but even stopping and standing near them while I waited felt like an infringement, an invasion of whatever private, terrible thing had happened to them. I wrapped myself into my coat and turned my back, hoping they would forget me altogether.

"Come on," he said sharply, once the hospital paperwork had been signed, and I followed them downstairs and out to the frozen parking lot and got into their car. He opened the door for his wife, and she stood from the wheelchair and let him ease her into the passenger seat in front of me. "I'll be right back," he said. His voice was gentle with her, and he seemed to touch her too carefully, awkwardly, the way I thought he would have to try to hold the tiny handle of a china teacup with his big hand.

I watched through the window as he wheeled the chair back across the icy pavement, taking big, sliding steps. He had turned on the car before leaving us, turned the heat up so that it whirred and the windows began to cloud. I thought I could smell birth still on his wife's body, the dark smell of it, though I knew she would have been bathed before leaving the hospital, she would have had fresh clothes to put on for the trip home. I wondered what it was that had happened. If they'd left the baby upstairs, because it was early and small, or because it had any one of the number of problems I'd seen since starting in labor and delivery—a hole in the heart, weak lungs, jaundice. Or if their baby would not be coming home at all. I considered opening the door and getting out, walking the rest of the way home, cut free.

I thought of Amanda and Mr. Pederson. I had told her the story that my mother told me every winter: Mr. Pederson cutting off his own index finger with an ice saw, the way it bled on the ice, through the brown wool of his mitten, and how they had to leave the ice then and carry him into town in the wagon, the finger wrapped up in waxed paper from someone's picnic lunch.

There was more to my mother's story that I hadn't told Amanda, though, a part I kept to myself. They had gone to the river to cut ice, squares of ice each as big as a child, that would go in the icehouse on a bed of sawdust (or on a bad year, hay). The ice would last that way late into the summer, until July or August, and on very hot days my mother would be allowed to go with the ice pick to chip a piece off and let it melt in her mouth and down the insides of her arms.

The river was frozen through, like every year, and they pulled the wagons down and took a picnic. There'd been snow in the morning, so the river was white, footprinted with the tracks of the men already cutting at the ice and the children running, sliding in their boots or on the blades of their skates. When my mother brushed the snow away in a spot, she could see the river below, solid, but still familiar brown, the flecks of algae and silt, the splayed fronds of river grasses reaching up. Above, the bare branches of river alders and birch bent down, and the long whips of willow trees, stripped of their leaves and sheathed in casings of ice.

My mother always sighed when she told the story, a slight rise and fall in her breath, the way it seemed the branches of the trees might rise and fall as she moved beneath them, the way they would hold her a moment, then release her, making room for her child-body to slip through. When she sighed, I believed I could hear the saw blades pulling out of the ice, hear the quiet slicing of my mother's skates down the center of the long, frozen river, while below her the silent, deeper current that never freezes kept moving.

I looked out at the blaze of the ice skinning the hospital parking lot, the way the ice flashed with the white and red of headlights as other cars pulled in and drove away.

In the front seat of the car, Mrs. Vagen shifted so that she could see me. "My husband says you like stars," she said. And then, letting go of her breath, she started, "Cassiopeia. Pegasus. Andromeda. Orion."

We took a back way home, a way I hadn't taken before, downtown and over the bridge, and then along the beach, through the fog, which seemed whiter and more cottony than it had ever been. I could not see the water. I could not see the line of familiar houses or the wet tops of spruce trees leaning along the road. "I don't know this way," I said. But in the front they were both quiet, and the car kept moving. There were slicks of frost on the pavement, and the tires swerved and skid until Mr. Vagen finally eased off the gas, rolling the weight of us forward slowly in what I trusted was the direction of home.

Surfacing

Miriam had drunk too much already by the time the boat eased into the water. While the men backed the truck down the launching ramp, she and Julia sat on the sand. Julia had packed wine, but no glasses, and when she offered the bottle, Miriam drank from it, one long swallow and then another. It was hot on the beach, and her mouth felt dry and gritty. The wine had a bitter aftertaste, though, and she thought she spotted sand at the bottom of the bottle.

There was a glare where they sat, the sun flashing off the blue-black surface of the Sound and striking the sand so that it seemed to sparkle. Miriam raised a hand to her forehead, as if looking out at something, a bird or the white buoys that ducked and bobbed far out in the water, but in the shade of her hand she closed her eyes. Beneath her arms, she could feel her deodorant melting. There would be white half-moons of it dried to the fabric of her blouse when she took it off later, the sweet, dank smell of her body still warm inside her clothes.

Miriam turned to watch the men unwinding the spools of cable that held the boat to the trailer. The metal trailer groaned and creaked, held the boat a moment before letting it slip into the water. She felt the bottle in her hand again, still cold from Julia and Ted's refrigerator. Not far out, another boat was anchored and lilting with the movement of the waves—the only other boat on the water. Past it, across the Sound, the islands floated behind a shimmer of heat and salt, and beyond them, the Olympics. Miriam pressed her heels into the sand, felt heat seep into the skin of her feet and ankles, passed the bottle back.

Miriam and Kurt had been out with Julia and Ted only a few times before, the first time a long evening at a play that Miriam could not remember well now. A story about a man and his dying son that had reminded her slightly of the Abraham and Isaac story she'd learned as a child, but not as good, not as simple.

At the coffeehouse Julia led them to after the play, Kurt said the script was *subtle*. Miriam looked at him as he said it. *Of course,* she thought. *That is of course something he would say.* He'd ordered black coffee (though at home he never took it without sugar and milk), and Miriam watched the way he cupped his hands around the coffee mug while he spoke about the play, his palms close against the hot mug and the tips of his thin fingers reddening. "I think it was very subtle," he said. He raised his eyes to meet Julia's, and Miriam watched as Julia held his stare. "Very," Kurt paused, "oblique."

The second time they'd met, they'd gathered for dinner at Julia and Ted's apartment downtown. Julia and Ted lived on the fourth floor of one of the older but renovated buildings, in a two-bedroom with a slight view of the Sound from the northwest-facing window. Julia took Miriam's elbow when they arrived and led her through the apartment. "The tour," Julia said. "I always want to see the whole house when I'm invited to dinner, so I'll just show you around now."

Miriam could smell Julia's perfume as she let herself be led through the small hallways and whitewashed rooms. It smelled like ginger and grass, and when Miriam took off her sweater later that evening at home, she found the scent still in the yarn where Julia's hand had been.

The men called to them from the water, and Julia stood up, brushed the sand from her shorts, and held out a hand to Miriam. They would have to wade in to their knees and then climb up the four or five feet of the narrow ladder Kurt was holding. "We might have just slipped on board to begin with," Julia said. Her speech was soft already and her steps in the sand too big. She hadn't dropped Miriam's hand after helping her stand up off of the sand, and her fingers were warm and interlaced with Miriam's as they walked.

At the water, Julia let her husband lift her to his shoulders for a boost, then scrambled over the edge of the boat to the deck. Kurt held the ladder still as Miriam climbed up after her. From the top of the ladder, Miriam could see out over the boat to where the sky and water seemed to waver and merge, a band of yellow-green haze in the distance. There was the thick, fishy smell of kelp rising up out of the water beneath her. She stood on the top rung of the ladder and closed her eyes a moment before easing her leg above the railing and pushing herself over onto the deck.

The night they'd gone to Julia and Ted's apartment, Julia had served bottle after bottle of what she said was her favorite wine, a thin Chardonnay that slipped like water down Miriam's throat. She drank too much then, too, and had wandered along the hallway to the bathroom several times during the course of the evening. There was a small mirror above the sink—not the original, but a round, feminine-looking, wicker-framed mirror that Julia had hung—and Miriam leaned in close to it, watched the wide circles of her pupils expand in the dark. Tea candles burned in glass votives on the rim of the bathtub and the back of the toilet. Yellowed light made the walls move around Miriam as she ran cold water over her hands and touched them to the back of her neck and the damp flat of her chest just beneath her collarbones.

She looked at her face in the mirror. It was thin, bluish in the dips beneath her eyes, as if she might not have slept enough lately, or could stand to start taking vitamins. Her face, Miriam knew, was that of a woman who had reached middle age. Julia's face, on the other hand, was still young, girlish. She had seemed to glow from across the dinner table. As she'd cut the roast, a line of sweat had beaded on her forehead, dampening the fine hairs that grew there. She had the kind of full lips—full like those of the Madonna in old, museum oil paintings—that made Miriam want to bite things. When they had first arrived at the apartment and Julia had leaned in to hug her greeting, Miriam had wanted to bite her. She'd clenched her jaw around the desire.

The men appeared over the edge of the boat deck, and Ted sat down at the steering wheel to start the motor. It was only a small boat, something they used now and then when it wasn't raining. They paid for an extra parking spot in their apartment's garage in order to store it. Ted fished from the boat, and Julia liked to sunbathe, she'd said, bring a book and read in the sun. Her legs were a smooth, suede tan already. Sometimes they anchored the boat and slept in the tight room just beneath the deck. When Julia stood up and opened the tiny trapdoor down to it, Miriam saw how uncomfortable the room looked, cramped and poorly lit, only a heap of blankets and two pillows on the carpeted floor. She didn't imagine it bothered Ted and Julia to sleep there together, though.

"Go on." Julia smiled, and the glare from the deck flashed against her teeth. She nudged Kurt. "Go on and see how small it is." She had taken her tee shirt off, left it wadded on her chair, and was in her bikini top, a line of white, untanned skin just showing from beneath the strap on her left shoulder.

Kurt stepped toward her, then back again. He looked to Miriam. "No," he said. "No, you go ahead."

Julia slipped down into the darkness herself. A cool draft rose up out of the lower room and washed over Miriam's ankles.

Ted had driven them out from the shoreline, and the other boat she had seen from the beach was not far from where Ted cut the engine to let them drift. Without the noise of the motor, there was only the sound of the water slapping below. Miriam squinted out at the other boat. There was a family on board, and the children were taking turns jumping from the boat to the water. The littlest had bright, inflatable water wings on each of his arms. He jumped only when the taller boy did, their heads disappearing beneath the black sheet of water for a moment, then bobbing back to the top in a commotion of sputtering and splashing. Miriam watched them jump and disappear, jump and disappear, until her eyes felt heavy and burned from looking at the water.

Miriam and Kurt did not have children. She had never miscarried, never even been late enough to worry. She had never, not for an imagined instant, been anybody's mother. There had been a while, at the beginning, when they'd talked about a baby—when *Kurt* had talked about a baby. But the time had not been right, and after that, the question had not come up again.

It was lightening. Miriam was just herself as she had always been. Her life had gone on, uninterrupted, without invasion.

When she was out, buying groceries or at the library, the sounds of other people's children irritated her. The shrill scream of a child's tantrum could shoot like a spear of ice through her head. When they whined at the checkout for a pack of gum, she very often nearly bought one herself to give to them, rather than continuing to listen to their bellowing.

"I'd like to have children," Julia had said at the dinner. "I'd be a great mother." She raised her wineglass to her mouth and pressed the rim to the flesh of her bottom lip, then lowered it without drinking. "Someday later, though," she added. "When I'm older, and I don't care so much about things anymore." She smiled, lifted the glass again, and swallowed the last of her wine.

Miriam could imagine Julia's children. They'd be quick and small-bodied. They'd be beautiful.

Miriam listened to the splashes of the children jumping from the other boat into the water. Later, their parents would bring the boat in to shore and take them home, carry them upstairs and tuck them into beds with red or blue sheets. Their hair would be stiff with salt, and there would be sand between their toes and in the swirls of their small ears. Miriam wondered how old they were. Across the water they jumped in again, and she leaned back in her chair and closed her eyes.

Julia emerged from the trapdoor holding two more bottles of wine. She had taken her shorts off downstairs, and walked onto the deck in just her bathing suit. She stepped past Miriam and slipped herself into the small space between the two men on the deck's bench. "Open these," she said, and handed each man a bottle. The sun had begun to slide toward the greenish haze of the horizon. It hung low, still above the Olympics, but less bright. Its light poured golden down the long eastern slopes of the mountains and glazed the tips of the waves a honeyed brown.

Miriam watched Kurt squeeze the wine bottle between his thighs to steady it as he worked the wings of the corkscrew Julia had given him. He was bare chested, the wiry gray hairs that crept in a streak up to his neck silvered in the sun. He had tucked his shirt into the back of his waistband and was sitting on it, the fabric loose and hanging behind his legs like a funny half-shirt.

A diaper, Miriam thought and grinned. Ted had gotten his cork out right away and had thrown it out into the water before giving the bottle back to Julia to drink from. The two of them seemed not to notice Kurt's flailing. He flapped the arms of the corkscrew up and down, up and down, until finally the cork popped and bounced across the deck.

Julia laid her palm against his thigh and took the bottle. "That's okay," she said, and winked as she got up to collect the cork. "Happens to a lot of men." She tossed the cork into the water and laughed at her joke, then sat back down between the men and ran her hand back and forth along Kurt's kneecap and the cuff of his shorts as she talked to Ted.

Miriam turned her head. She didn't want to know if he was already sleeping with Julia, or just considering it.

Julia looked up suddenly. "I'm hungry," she declared. "I'm hungry, and no one thought to bring food. There's no food on board."

"Have more wine." Ted drank from one of the bottles, then tipped it for Julia, like feeding a baby. She puffed out her cheeks to hold it, but wine spilled from the sides of her mouth and dripped down her neck and chest. Miriam waited for Ted to lick it from her skin, or for Kurt to, but the men both just stared as Julia sputtered and wiped at it herself.

There may have been one other woman before Julia. Alene, the wife of a man Kurt knew from work. The four of them had gone to dinner too, several times, to a swanky restaurant downtown that Alene had chosen. A place that served things like salmon dolloped with hollandaise and capers, salads leafy with dandelion and escarole. Alene always seemed impressed.

Once they went to a place on the pier. Alene's husband insisted on paying, and so Miriam ordered a lobster pasta, two glasses of a wine label she couldn't pronounce, and a chocolate mousse. She watched Alene as she ate. Alene's hair was thick and red and wavy. She had full hips and wore skirts that shifted around her body when she moved, danced at her ankles as she walked. When she ate, she licked dribbles of dressing from her lips, flicked her tongue out quickly between bites.

Kurt may not have noticed her at all, Miriam wasn't sure. She wasn't sure how she felt about him if he hadn't.

Miriam took the bottle of wine Kurt held out to her and finished it. She squeezed her hand around the slim neck and thought of throwing it into the waves. She would stand up and take a step back to throw it. The bottle would arc up over the boat deck and the water, and in her vision, it would rise above the line of the bluing mountains before sliding down and down through the yellowed air to float on the surface of the Sound.

She set the bottle beneath her chair. The sun was perched at the crest of the horizon, about to slip from the sky.

"Well, I guess that's the end of it," Julia said. She pulled her lips down into a childish pout, then grinned. "Actually, honey," she said, turning to Ted, "I think there might be just one more bottle downstairs." When she spoke to him, she put her face very near his, their noses nearly brushing against one another, pecking a bit, like silly birds.

"I'll go." Miriam stood up. The motion of the boat swayed her, and her deck chair slid forward as she folded her fingers down over it. She stood straighter and reached for the boat railing instead. "Where is the wine?"

"It's just behind the place where we keep the extra blankets. In that cupboard. Right behind that door." Julia had put her head on Kurt's shoulder and closed her eyes. She pointed in the direction of the trapdoor and wagged her hand. "I know there's one more down there."

"I'm not sure we need more," Kurt said. His eyes widened as Julia's hand dropped back down on his thigh. She kept her eyes closed and fingered the fabric of his shorts until he eased her weight onto Ted and got up to take Miriam's empty chair. "No, I think we're done for, folks."

Miriam narrowed her eyes at the back of his head. *Folks* was exactly the kind of word he liked to use.

"Here," Ted said, letting Julia's body down onto the bench and wadding up his tee shirt as a pillow. "I'll show you where it is. Julia's not going to be much help with directions right now." He crossed the deck and led Miriam down into the lower room.

It was cool there. The air was thin and salty with the smell of clothes and towels damp with seawater and left to dry. A window of thick glass bubbled out and let a small circle of light into the darkness. The room was paneled in walnut-colored manufactured wood, the kind Miriam's parents had put up in their rec room when she went away to college. If you tapped on it, it gave out a false, plastic kind of sound that betrayed it as something other than wood. All around the little room were cupboards, also covered in paneling so that they seemed to blend in, to disappear in the way of hidden doors in old novels. Miriam folded her legs beneath herself and sat down on the floor where the blankets and pillows of the makeshift bed had been rumpled. The cool air seemed to clear her head, to wash the alcoholic, gauzy feeling from her tongue.

"It's nice down here," she said. She lay back on the pillows and inhaled the grassy scent of Julia's perfume. "Do you two sleep here often?" She thought about how lovely Julia must look sprawled out on top of the mess of pillows. Like a glossy photograph for cologne or shoes, the kind that always features a group of young people lying on tartan blankets somewhere along the Atlantic coastline.

Ted reached up to a top cupboard and brought down the bottle he'd been looking for. "There's one more still back there," he said, "but I don't think we'll tell her about it."

Miriam didn't actually know much of anything at all about Ted. Other than that he worked in Kurt's building—an accountant or a data analyst—and that he seemed very like Kurt, in the way he dressed and spoke and moved. He was neither short nor tall, and he parted his hair a little farther to left than seemed normal, to cover the bit of a bald spot beginning at the crown of his head. He must have had braces as a kid, she thought. His teeth were amazingly straight. He was, she imagined, maybe ten years Julia's senior, maybe twelve. No older than Miriam herself was, and not much older than Kurt. Sometimes Ted reminded Miriam so much of Kurt, in fact, that the two seemed nearly interchangeable in her mind, one perhaps a carbon copy of the other.

Ted held the bottle over his head. "Ta da," he said.

On their first date, Kurt had picked Miriam up wearing a suit and tie, then took her to a fish-and-chips restaurant near the piers. It was a theme restaurant, all of the waiters dressed like pirates with eye patches and feathers in their hats like Captain Hook, all of the waitresses like mermaids, with green sequined skirts that ended at their knees in a big, fabric flipper. The menu listed dishes like *Captain's Cove Clam Chowder* and *Green Salad with Treasure Island Dressing*. There was sand on the floor, and the tables were raw wood, stained and abused to look as if they'd just washed in.

When Miriam ran her hand along the table, the wood peeled, and a splinter stuck in her palm. Kurt took an ice cube from his water and slipped it along the inside of her wrist and palm until the skin of her hand felt numb. With the sharp point of his tie tack, he lifted the skin.

"Do all men know how to do this?" she asked. She remembered her father removing slivers of bark from her hand as a child, picking rocks from a skinned knee with the careful precision of a surgeon.

Kurt smiled, eased the splinter out.

She would marry him, she was certain then. She would ensure that he was happy.

Ted sat down beside Miriam on the pillows. "First sip?" He uncorked the bottle and offered it to her.

The sound of the water outside was muffled from where Miriam sat. The breeze had blown the trapdoor nearly closed, and Miriam could hear that Kurt and Julia were singing up on the deck, though the words of their song were fat and unclear to her, as if her ears were plugged, or she had slid beneath the surface of the water. She closed her eyes and felt Ted lie back beside her. She could smell the wine on his breath as he breathed out, the fruity, medicinal scent of his sunscreen. When she pushed herself up onto her elbow to look at him, he seemed to be sleeping. She leaned over his body and put her face close to his as Julia had done, touched the tip of her nose to his own, and his eyes opened. She thought he might laugh, but instead he kissed her.

The night they were married, Miriam had undressed and gotten into the hotel bed to wait for Kurt. She could hear him in the bathroom, brushing his teeth, gargling, then spitting out his mouthwash. He was trying. She knew that. She knew he would come to her warm, his mouth wet on her neck and eager. He would put his arms around her and breathe into her ear.

She pulled the sheets up over her shoulders. Already the bed seemed crowded. She was suddenly annoyed at how much of it she was expected to share.

Miriam sat up and shoved herself back against the wall of the boat. "Stop," she said to Ted. "That's good enough." She reached her hand up beneath her shirt and straightened herself out, ran her fingers through her hair and stood up. "I'll take that wine up to them," she said.

On the deck, Kurt and Julia were still singing, a song about margaritas, though they could only remember the chorus and kept repeating it, loud and out of key. Miriam touched the back of Kurt's neck with the wine bottle and leaned to kiss his cheek.

"Do you want your chair back?" He stood up and took the wine from her, tucked it behind the heap of lifejackets and rescue rings piled near the railing. "I think we've had enough up here," he said. He spoke in a parental tone, and widened his eyes at Miriam, as if the two of them shared the responsibility of keeping the wine from Julia's sight. Julia was back at the beginning of the chorus and didn't hear him.

Across the water, the people on the other boat seemed to be cleaning up for the day. The line of buoys Miriam had seen the children playing with earlier had been dragged in and looped up over the deck, and the mother had pulled her shorts and tank top back on over her suit. The littlest boy stood on the railing, his yellow trunks still soaked and his arms flapping, free of the water wings he'd been wearing. He wrapped his arms around himself and turned his head back toward his mother. Miriam watched the mother point her finger, giving orders. She watched the little boy shake his head and jump.

The boy's head disappeared beneath the black shine of the water.

Miriam sat forward in her chair. The sun had just slid behind the mountains and glinted there, rays red and silver and white, streaming out from between the peaks and blinding her. She squinted and waited for the boy's head to bob back up. He'd been below a long time. Miriam counted the seconds. *Fifty, fifty-two, fifty-eight.* She looked for the flash of his yellow shorts beneath the surface. "Drowning," she said quietly to herself.

She imagined jumping in after him, the needles of cold and the pressure as the walls of water closed in around her, as water flooded in and invaded her lungs. She imagined the desperate groping as her hands failed to find his body in the darkness anyway. *Ninety-eight, ninety-nine,* she counted. She breathed deeply between the seconds, and she was not sorry she could breathe.

The boy's wet head popped up, and Miriam watched him paddle to the boat's ladder, swing himself back up onto the deck. She let out the breath she had been hoarding in her chest.

"What happened to that wine?" Julia asked. She stopped her song and raised her head. Her hair had come loose from its ponytail on one side and flopped there next to her ear. Around her eyes, her mascara was soft and sooty, and in the poor light, her makeup looked sallow, jaundiced where the line of her jaw met her neck. She smiled. "Did everyone forget about the wine?"

Ted had come up and was sitting with his back against the wall of the deck, his legs stretched out in front of him. He met Kurt's eyes and nodded. "There weren't any more bottles down there, Jules," he said to his wife. "You're out of luck."

"What do you say we call it anyway," Kurt said, and grinned. "We'll be in the dark in a few minutes." He moved to stand behind Miriam, rested his palms on her shoulders.

She let him hold her there, beneath his hands, and felt the light weight of his fingers, the heels of his palms, and the way they gave up their warmth to her, the slight heat passing from his skin, through her blouse to her own. She eased under his grasp, stood there with him as Ted started up the motor and began back toward the shore.

The Picnic

"Quiet now," my mother said. "And don't act put on. Vivian notices every little flaw." She walked ahead of me a few paces, her handbag pumping back and forth at her elbow. On her other arm, a canvas sack bulged with our picnic. All morning she had been feeding me manners, readying me for our meeting with my aunt. As we crested the top of the hill and crossed the street to the wrought-iron gate of the park, she stopped, turned to face me, and laid her hand on my shoulder. "Leigh," she said. She fixed her eyes on me, smiled weakly. "This will be a fine visit, won't it?" She waited for me to nod, then smoothed the front of her slacks and settled the picnic bag up higher on her shoulder. "It will be a very good visit."

I had met my Aunt Vivian only a few times, though she was the kind of woman who made an impression. She was never in one place long, and always met us with gifts from wherever it was she'd just been: chocolates from Switzerland once, and another time, just for me, an enamel box the size of a pincushion, with a hinged lid, and inside, a tooth.

"Good God, Viv," my mother had said, when I opened the box and dropped the tiny tooth into my palm. It was hard as a pebble, the color of mother-of-pearl.

Vivian turned to me, beaming, the dangles of her earrings swinging below her earlobes, catching light. "It's real," she said. "They say if a woman has one of these, she won't ever find the desire to see her own baby's teeth." She looked to my mother then. "If I'd known about this before, we might have been able to save you too."

Now, crossing through the park with my mother, I squeezed the picnic blanket to myself and tried to keep to my mother's slow pace. She had said Vivian would meet us at the conservatory, which I'd imagined like the conservatories in books: domed and glass-walled and spilling over with palm trees and birds-of-paradise and thick-skinned, hungry Venus's-flytrap plants. This seemed to me the perfect place for meeting Aunt Vivian, who had been to the tropics and had stories about drinking straight from a coconut, about lying on a beach in a country where the ocean was as warm as bath water.

"Why don't you just come to the house instead?" my mother had asked her over the phone. "Why don't you stay a few days? Jim is out of town this week anyhow. It will just be Leigh and me here at the house." She stood at our kitchen sink as she spoke to Vivian, and from where I sat behind her, my mother looked like a mother, full in her hips and dowdy. At nights, getting ready for bed, I often sat on the edge of my mother's bathtub and talked to her as she washed her face and rubbed small circles of white cold cream across her cheekbones, then undressed and slipped her nightgown over her head. Her body was soft, dimpled just above her backside, her hips lined with fine pale stretch marks like hairline fractures on a porcelain dish.

I listened to her argue with Vivian a moment more about where to meet, then turned away from her and left the room.

Later, my mother came to find me to say that Vivian wouldn't be staying at the house. She had only the one afternoon, and then she'd be gone again. "This is what she does," my mother said. "She leaves. It's why she'll never be anything but alone."

In the park the grass was still wet with overnight rain, and as we walked, it soaked through the fabric of my shoes and wet the cuffs of my mother's trousers. There were great circular gardens planted here and there, each named by a metal plaque sunk into the dirt. I ran from my mother to stand in front of each of the signs, then called out to her what I read from them. "Queen Elizabeth's Tulip Garden," I turned to holler at her, and ran the few feet to the next circle of blooms, this one named less romantically, "The Rose Garden." Through the canopy of oak and evergreen branches above my head I could see squares of blue-white sky, the color of a robin's egg, and from between their leaves and needles, filaments of sunlight filtered down into the park.

"A bad year for blossoms," my mother said, when I came to her side again. She looked back toward the tulips, which were browned, most of the petals already on the ground, losing their color. "They're perennials though, you know. The bulbs just stay in the ground and come back the next year, stronger, maybe." She set her eyes on the conservatory, which had just appeared ahead of us, and kept walking.

The last time Vivian had come to visit, she'd appeared unexpectedly, waiting for me in the front yard of my school after classes let out. I didn't recognize her at first, and stood staring a moment, my school bag slumped down at my feet, my jacket coming off my shoulder. Vivian crossed the lawn and straightened the jacket, tidied the collar of my blouse, and pushed my hair back over my shoulders. "You look beat," she said, and grinned. "Come with me."

That day she was driving a pale blue convertible, the old kind, and we rode with the top down, the wind whipping our hair around our faces and blowing my eyes dry so that I had to squint. Vivian had sunglasses, of course, and at the first stoplight, bent down and pulled two scarves from her purse. She handed one to me. "Tie this around your head," she said, and slipped hers around her own head, knotting it at the nape of her neck. "We'll look like fashion plates," she said. "Like Nancy Drew. She had a blue convertible, if I remember right." She looked at me and grinned as I adjusted the scarf over my hair. "Just like Nancy."

I smiled back at her. I wanted to tell her that it had been years since I'd read those books, ages. But I just knotted my scarf as Vivian had knotted hers and sat back against my seat.

Vivian drove through downtown and out across the bridge to the west side of the city. I'd been there before with my mother, running errands, but as we passed the straight rows of two-story houses with their cement walks all the same and their round rhododendron bushes blooming red and purple beside their front doors, it seemed like a new city, unfamiliar and awake.

We stopped at an ice-cream shop for cones, then walked along the waterfront eating them. I hadn't untied my scarf from my head, and believed I looked at least thirteen with it on, walking beside my aunt with the legs of my jeans rolled up, balancing from rock to rock down the beach, my bare feet toeing the froth as waves lapped in and out.

"Are you coming for dinner then?" I asked.

"Your mother doesn't even know I'm in town." Vivian held my outstretched hand, steadying me on the slippery rocks. She stopped and turned to face me. I couldn't see her eyes behind her sunglasses. "We won't tell her about this," she said. "This kind of spontaneity is not something your mother understands. I know you tell her everything, but this we'll keep between us."

I stepped down from the rock and let go of her hand. I had already been saving in my mind the things I wanted to tell my mother when I got home: the way the inside of Vivian's car smelled like vanilla, how the boy at the ice-cream store had forgotten to charge us for my scoop of peppermint because of the way Vivian had looked at him over the counter. I wanted to tell my mother about walking on the beach, about how Vivian made our city seem foreign and divine.

"I understand," I said, and sat down, my cone finished, to put on my shoes.

When we reached the conservatory, Vivian was waiting for us. She stood up and waved, and my mother lifted her hand and waved back. "She's early," my mother said. "She'll tell us we've kept her waiting." My mother walked ahead of me toward Vivian, set the picnic bag down at her feet, and hugged her sister.

"Martha," Vivian said. Over my mother's shoulder, she winked at me, and I flushed. "Martha, you didn't have to bring a lunch."

"It is a picnic, isn't it?" My mother pulled back and stooped to lift the bag again. "What would we have eaten if I hadn't brought it?"

Vivian's arms were full of her coat, her tiny handbag, and nothing else. She shrugged. "Always the practical thinker, your mother," she said to me, and winked again. She laced her arm through my mother's, and the two of them walked into the conservatory ahead of me.

The building was glass and domed, as I had imagined, but inside, it was green with the same local plants I'd seen before in the nurseries and garden shops: daffodils leaning on their tall, slim shoots near the footpath; a show of lilies and hydrangea in the corner; an olive tree in the center, crowned in long, glossy leaves, only domestically exotic.

Vivian and my mother walked the path in front of me, speaking in low tones I could not fully hear. My mother was shorter than Vivian by almost six inches and not nearly as slim. She had her long hair curled, and in the humid warmth of the conservatory, the curls stretched out and lengthened, undoing themselves. Vivian slipped her hand from my mother's arm and touched my mother's hair, squeezed a handful of it, so that when she let go, all of the curl was flattened, ratty looking.

"Viv," my mother said, irritated. She stepped away, putting her own hand to her head and smoothing the mess Vivian had left.

"You should wear it straight," Vivian said. "It looks better when you wear it natural." She laughed, looked back at me. "When we were girls she slept with juice cans fastened to her head so she could have the curls. She had to sleep sitting upright. You remember that, Mart? You remember sitting up all night like that?"

My mother straightened up, tugged the strap of the picnic bag tight against her shoulder. "That's a ridiculous thing to bring up," she said. "Vivian's not telling you, Leigh, how she once burned off the last four inches of her hair, trying to iron it as straight as mine."

"Well," Vivian said, with a long breath. She and my mother rounded the bend in the path and headed back outside to the grass.

My mother told me once that Vivian showed up at the hospital the day I was born. "Your father called her," she said. She smiled. "He called everyone, but Vivian was the one who showed up."

Vivian had been in California, my mother said. Or maybe out of the country. She didn't know. Vivian never called to say where she was going or when she'd be back, because there had never been a place to come back to. "She liked it that way," my mother said when she told me. "You know, you can keep above everything if you never stay put, the dailiness and the responsibility." My mother looked away from me. "The boredom. Transcendence through avoidance. That's how Vivian lives."

But Vivian had appeared at the door of my mother's hospital room just after my birth, her arms full of packages, a bundle of pink roses wrapped in brown paper. "It was silly," my mother said, "but somehow, lying in the hospital bed with you beside me, I felt like

I might never see the outside again." She laughed. "Isn't that silly? The roses were welcome, though, at that moment very welcome."

My father left the room for lunch, and Vivian sat on the side of my mother's bed and picked me up. "She was worried you'd be sick on her blouse," my mother went on. "It was silk, she said, from China. Red, with a peony, or some kind of Chinese flower imprinted on the shoulder."

At this part of the story, I didn't want to hear about Vivian's blouse. I wanted my mother to tell me what Vivian had said about me. I wanted to know how my aunt's face had looked when she held me, and if it had seemed, for just an instant, that she wished to trade places with my mother. I wanted that look from Vivian, for my mother's sake, and for my own.

Sometimes, after one of the adolescent arguments I was having with my mother more and more often, I closed myself into my room and opened the enamel box Vivian had given to me and imagined a life as her daughter. There would be beauty all around me always, and that feeling of wide awareness I'd had with her the day she picked me up from school. I liked imagining it—my life with Vivian. But once the fantasy passed I was always left guilty, sorry that I had thought it, and that part of me still wanted it to be true.

"You know you were named for her," my mother said, closing her story about my birth. She got up from the couch where we'd been sitting. My father would be home soon, and I followed behind her into the kitchen to help her start supper. I took three plates from the cupboard and stacked them on the table, setting it as she went on.

"Vivian looked at you and said, 'She's got my name, right?'" As if it were a given." My mother turned on the faucet, dipped the silver basin of a pot beneath it so that the rush of water bubbled up and over the lip before she turned it off. "She had so little then, really. Or that's how it seemed to me. So I said, 'Sure, she's named for you. Leigh.'"

"But her name is Vivian," I said as I straightened the napkins beside each plate and laid out the silverware. The evening light coming in through the window lit my mother where she stood, looking out at the lawn beyond the house. It shone through the row of glass bottles she kept on the window ledge and painted her, prisms of red and gold and green on the skin of her neck and against her hair.

"Leigh. Like Vivien Leigh, the actress. That's who Vivian was named for. That's where I got your Leigh." My mother turned to look at me and smiled, the light still in her hair. "Not really like her at all."

I pushed back in my chair and got up, left her to fix dinner by herself.

Outside, in the park, we found a square of grass in the sun, and I shook out and spread our blanket. Vivian sat down on one side of me. She set her handbag and coat at her feet and curled her knees up beneath her. She'd worn a skirt, blue linen, and she shifted herself, trying to keep it from wrinkling.

My mother sat on the other side of me and began pulling our lunch from the canvas sack. "Sandwiches," she said, and passed them to me. She'd baked the bread herself the night before, late, after I had already gone to bed. I heard her in the kitchen and got up to find her in her nightgown, her arms white to the elbows with flour, only the yellow light from the porch lamp outside coming into the room through the window. Isn't it dark? I asked. When she looked up, she shook her head over the motion of her kneading. Go back to bed, she told me.

"My mother made this bread," I said to Vivian. I wanted to shame them both.

Vivian took a sandwich from my hand and peeled back the waxed paper, bit into the bread, and when she'd swallowed, looked to my mother. "You could have bought some, Mart. I could have stopped at a bakery on the way."

My mother sniffed and passed me a glass jar of cucumber slices floating in vinegar and dill, and a red netted bag, heavy with three oranges. "We wouldn't have had bread then. We'd be eating turkey on lettuce." She opened a paper napkin over her lap and one over mine, dropping the canvas sack in the center of the blanket. "There are more napkins inside, if you didn't bring your own," she said to Vivian.

Vivian ate her sandwich and looked away from us.

Across the lawn, a pair of pigeons stood waiting for us to get up and leave them our crumbs. They fixed their red eyes on us, and now and then opened their wings and flapped at one another, bobbed heads and chortled, then settled again and sat together quietly. Beyond them, over the rise of our hill, were the peaks of the evergreens at the edge of the park, their needles shimmering, metallic in the sunlight, silvered and sharp against the white noon sky.

My mother slipped an orange from the bag and dug the tip of a butter knife under its skin. "You could stay tonight, at the house," she said. "If you're in town tonight, it would be fine." She looked up at Vivian. "Jim's gone for the week. I think I mentioned that on the phone."

Vivian crumpled her waxed paper into a ball and reclined back onto her elbow, stretching her legs long, toeing off her pumps. She closed her eyes. "They do that," she said. "Leave."

"He's only left for the week, Viv."

Vivian shifted to face me. "You know your mother and father amaze me. How many years have they been married?"

I looked to my mother.

"Fourteen," she said, and leaned across me to drop the rind of her orange back into the bag. It had left an iridescence like fish scales on her palms, and she wiped them against her napkin. She tore a section from the orange and bit into it. "Leigh doesn't want my life," she said to my aunt. "Counting years is like counting sheep."

Vivian reached out, and I felt her fingers in my hair. "Yes," she said. "But maybe you end up with a dream."

The day Vivian picked me up from school, we drove home from the beach with the top up on the convertible. I held my backpack against my chest as she drove, watching the traffic lights change up ahead of us, the flow of cars, all of them but Vivian's headed back toward home.

"Where are you going after this?" I asked. "After you drop me off, where are you driving?" I wanted her to tell me she was going down the coast tonight, all the way to California, or north, to Vancouver, or to Anacortes, where the ferry takes off for the islands.

"This isn't even my car, honey," she said. "I'm taking it back to a friend's, the man who owns it. We'll go to dinner, and then I don't know what. There aren't really plans." She sat very straight behind the big steering wheel of the car, tensing every muscle in her arms to force the turns.

Later, when we reached my street, she pulled to the curb at the corner and stopped. "I'll let you out here," she said. "Have you worked up a good lie to tell your mother?" She smiled and kissed my forehead, waved to me as I climbed out, and quickly pulled away.

I hadn't thought about a lie and couldn't think of one all the way up my street. When I opened my front door, my mother was sitting on the couch. I dropped my book bag to the floor and looked up at her. "I'm sorry," I said.

She tapped the couch beside her. "Come sit with me," she said. Her voice was even and low, as it always was when she was angry, and I crossed the room to her and sat down.

In the other room, dinner was already cooking, and the house was full of the thick, homey scent of roast. I smelled it on her when she reached up and tugged Vivian's scarf from my hair, the bite of onions and spice sharp and familiar on my mother's fingers. I pulled away from her, and she stood up.

"This is nice," she said, running the scarf between her fingers, looking at the silk, the pattern of white and pink and yellow peonies blooming inside the blue border. She looked at me and held out the scarf for me to take. "You have good taste."

I didn't take the scarf from her, and she let go of it, so that it fluttered to the floor.

Later, in my room alone, I tied the scarf around my head again and looked at myself in the mirror until I didn't want to look anymore.

The picnic finished, we stood up and shook out the blanket, folding it together, Vivian and I on one end, my mother taking the other two corners. The grass on the hill had dried, and we walked down the hill carrying our shoes, then stopped at the gate to put them on.

It was two o'clock, and the sun was lower in the sky, almost milky through the clouds that had come in while we'd been beneath the trees. It would rain later that evening. I wondered if Vivian still had the blue convertible, or if she'd borrowed some other car this time. I thought of her driving in the rain to wherever it was she was going, an unfamiliar voice on the radio, the windows around her fogged, beads of rain on the glass stained red and yellow and green from the street lights.

"You should stay," I said, when my mother had started ahead of us down the block.

Vivian touched my arm but kept moving as if she hadn't heard me ask, and eventually caught up to my mother. The two of them walked together, their purses swinging on their arms, their feet finding the same rhythm a steady distance ahead of me.

It did begin to rain as we walked, just a sprinkling that dappled the street and wetted the air so that it smelled new again, green. Above the low clouds, there was sun and a line of blue that I could see stretched across the entire width of the sky, clear and certain and still bright, to the east and to the west alike.

Disappearing

It was not a short distance from Emmy's office to the hospital. But in the last few weeks before her sister's release date, she'd begun walking it every lunch hour. There was a flower shop on the corner just before Medical Street, a place with a green-tiled façade and a striped awning often drenched and hanging slack with rain. The shop did not have a front door exactly but was open to the street, a sort of permanent booth. Tin buckets of roses and gardenias, speckled lilies and frothy pink bundles of peonies and hydrangeas filled the shop and spilled out onto the sidewalk, spotting the wet concrete with shed petals. Emmy understood the sad point of the shop, the way it was positioned exactly across from the emergency room lobby. But she liked the smell of the flowers as she passed, the stark reds and yellows against the gray January slush on the sidewalk and street. She knew Ava liked having them in her room, to brighten it, and so on Mondays she stopped and bought a bunch before crossing the street and ascending the metal staircase to the EDU.

Once inside the hospital, she registered her name with the nurse and walked down the wide hallway to Ava's room to wait. Guests were not allowed to join patients in the dining room, especially not family members, whose presence would upset the meal hour. The doors to the dining room were always closed as Emmy passed it, drafts of the thick, solid food they served the patients slipping out into the hallway, stinking of vegetable matter, of cooked meat. Ava had complained that the food sank inside her once she ate it, that she could feel it in her middle like bricks, weighing her to the floor. "Touch my stomach," she said once, lifting her shirt to her chin. She put her own hand to it, slapped the skin there, hard, so that the five long lines of her fingers reddened on her belly, rose to welts. Emmy could see the fine bones of her sister's ribs protruding, the dark gooseflesh around her nipples. Ava had stopped wearing a bra when she lost her weight, her breasts shrunken, her thirty-five-year-old body sized back to adolescence. She wore heaps of tee shirts and turtlenecks and sweaters instead, all piled one over the other, so that her body was padded, insulated beneath the layers of fabric. When they hugged, Emmy couldn't always feel her sister beneath all of the clothes, just a soft, bodiless embrace, like squeezing a bundle of laundry to her chest.

In Ava's room, Emmy dumped last week's wilted daisies into the trash, poured the brown water from the vase into the sink, rinsed and refilled it, arranging this week's armful of peonies, Ava's favorites. She set them on the bedside table. The room smelled of vitamins, of rubbing alcohol, and of Ava's cheap, drugstore perfume. Ava had situated her things on the bureau at the foot of the bed and on the night table: a small stack of paperbacks; a journal and a pen; a glass snow globe that Emmy had bought for her birthday at a gift shop downtown. Emmy picked up the snow globe and tilted it once before setting it back down, so that the water slid up the glass sides of the globe, and the mirrored confetti showered down and piled again on the little plastic presents and drowned pink birthday cake inside.

Beside the snow globe, there was a photograph of Ava sitting on a terrace in Italy the spring she turned twenty-one and Emmy nineteen. They'd gone on the trip together, to celebrate, and it was Emmy who took the photo. Ava's problems first started that year, but she hadn't lost her weight yet in the picture. In the photograph she was slender but still full in her hips, her chest. Her face was that of a different, hardly recognizable sister.

"Hello," Ava said as she came in from the dining room. She kept her hands pressed to her stomach, leaned forward to kiss Emmy's cheek. When Emmy stood and reached out to hug her, she stepped away. "Bricks for lunch today," she said.

Emmy sat back down on the edge of the bed, smoothed her skirt. "I brought you flowers. The daisies were dead already. You have to do something about it when they start to die."

"You'll always just bring more," Ava said. She went into the bathroom, and Emmy heard the lock click from the other side. The nurses had asked her to report it to them if Ava did this, if she closed herself into the bathroom for very long after a meal. They'd told her to start banging on the door, to put her ear to it and listen, make sure Ava wasn't falling into old routines.

Emmy sat on the bed, though. She hummed softly beneath her breath the last song she'd heard on the radio that morning as she'd driven to work, the Beatles' "Eleanor Rigby." It was the kind of song whose tune stuck quickly in her mind once she'd heard it, but whose lyrics never would. She could only remember the part about the face in the jar by the door. *Who is it for?* She hummed and stood up, went to the window and tapped her fingers on the glass. The water came on in the bathroom. The toilet flushed, then flushed again.

Emmy pressed the tips of her fingers to the cool of the window, looked out at the street below, the tarpaper roof of the flower shop, the bare-limbed and dripping alders that stood in a line along the hospital lawn. The spread of the city was dull from this high up, soggy brown and gray, the last wet lumps of snow about to slide from the pitches of roofs. The sky was already darkening, the lights of the houses and buildings across town barely beginning to glitter. It would rain as she walked back to work. It looked like rain.

Ava opened the bathroom door and moved to sit down on the bed. "Are you trying to open those windows?" she asked. "None of them open on this wing."

"I'm just looking at the rain," Emmy said. She moved back to the bed, sat down beside her sister. Ava had mentioned the windows before, the captivity of the place. They'd taken her razor, she'd called once to complain. They'd taken the scissors she'd been keeping in the back of the bureau drawer for trimming her bangs, her letter opener. You knew all of their rules when you checked yourself in, Emmy always wanted to say, but she pressed her lips together, folded her hands into her lap, and shifted her weight on the mattress.

She'd never mentioned to the people in her office where she went on these lunch hours. They'd seen her tying on sneakers over her stockings and had smiled, raised their eyebrows appreciatively, as if she were a real trouper to be braving the January weather to get some exercise during her break. A few of the other women from the department would spend their lunches walking along the lake when the weather cleared again. Emmy had gone with them once or twice last spring, carrying shorts and a tee shirt in a canvas sack to work, then giving herself spit baths afterward from the washroom sink. It seemed embarrassing, though, returning to work in gym clothes, a mess. She didn't like the sweaty look of herself after the walks, the tangle the breeze near the water always made of her hair, and the clinging, outdoor odor she could smell on herself for the rest of the afternoon. So she had stopped walking with them, taking her lunch in her cubicle instead, reading novels while she ate her sandwich, sweeping the crumbs off onto the carpet when she finished.

"I need to ask you something today," Ava started. She picked at her fingernails as she spoke, tore at the red skin along the nail beds until she began to bleed. It was a habit she'd had since childhood, and whenever Emmy had asked her about it, reached out to touch her hands and remind her, Ava had promised to stop. *I just keep tearing myself to pieces, don't I*, she'd said once.

Ava stuck her finger in her mouth, sucked at it, then stood up to get a tissue from the box on the bureau. "Em," she said. "When I get out," she paused, directed her eyes to Emmy's as if to stress the weight of her question, "I'll need a place to stay for a while. Someone to help me, or maybe watch me, so that I don't—" She stopped again, pressed the tissue around her finger. A bright star of blood blossomed on the soft paper, and Emmy looked away. "Anyhow, I'm asking if could stay with you. At your place. For a while, until I sort myself out, get readjusted." Ava stepped back into the bathroom, and Emmy watched her through the open door, running water over the finger, wrapping it in a washcloth. She had lost nearly forty pounds in the few months before she'd come to the hospital, the most she'd ever lost all at once. She'd been slight before, and now, bent over the white sink, her pale hair pinned up and back as it was, she seemed frighteningly small, sharp.

"Of course," Emmy said. She stood up from the bed, gathered her coat and purse. "I should leave now. I have to walk back." She stood at the foot of the bed and waited for her sister to finish in the bathroom, to come out and hug her good-bye, thank her for the offer, the flowers.

"Okay," Ava said from the bathroom. She turned her face away from the mirror, smiled, turned back. "I'll see you tomorrow."

When she got home after work, Emmy took off her blouse and skirt, rolled her nylons into a ball, and ran a bath. Her hair had felt damp on her neck all afternoon from the walk back to her office, and it smelled to her of wet dog, of winter, and of Ava's peonies. She'd been thinking about a bath since the hospital.

She moved through the apartment naked as she waited for the tub to fill. It was a small apartment, and crowded. She had brought her own furniture when she'd moved in, and Linus had left his when he'd gone. Tables and bookshelves and floor lamps butted up against the walls and one another. A heap of coats and scarves and mittens lay at the foot of the short stairwell, overflow from the full hall closet. And beneath the bureau near the door were three umbrellas, a plastic rain hat, and the extra set of keys. Emmy passed these things, stepping over them as she walked.

At the kitchen table she went through her mail, sorted the bills from the coupons and advertisements, squared and stacked them on top of the piles of yesterday's mail and last month's catalogues. In the dark kitchen, she opened the refrigerator and pulled out a box of leftover pad thai, cut a chunk of fudge from the pan she had made the night before, poured a glass of sweet wine, and carried them all upstairs to the bathroom. The mirror had clouded with the heat of the bathwater, and she watched the pink shape of her body move across it as she came into the room. The fog blurred her figure, made her seem a swell of color on the mirror's surface. She set the food down on the counter and turned off the lights. Her arms were not as long as Ava's, but she reached them around herself, tightly, pushed the heels of her palms into the soft flesh just behind her shoulders, squeezed so that her breasts began to ache. She thought of Ava stepping away from her hug, and wondered again if her sister minded touching her. If she was too much like a pillow to hold, the excess of her body repulsive.

When Linus lived with her, he had often put his face to the cushion of her stomach while they lay in bed, rubbed his cheek on the pouch of skin there. "You're soft in all the right places," he'd say. "Built for comfort."

Emmy flipped the lights back on, slipped into the tub, and watched the water rise around her.

Saturday morning Emmy woke up early to snow. The apartment was quiet, any outside noise dampered, whited out by the few inches, and the light that came in through the windows was a heavy blue. She pulled on sweatpants and an old tee shirt, ate breakfast quickly, and settled herself in the center of the living room with a black plastic trash bag. If Ava would be staying, she would have to make room.

She and Ava had shared a bedroom once, as children, for just a month, during a visit from their mother's aunt. The aunt had slept in Emmy's room—she'd volunteered it—and Emmy had moved in with Ava. Ava's bedroom was big, with a bunk bed and an extra dresser for Emmy's clothes, but even so, Ava complained about the mess Emmy always made with her toys, about the way she wouldn't hang up her clothes, about the stink of her things in the room. "I can smell you," she'd say in the middle of the night. She'd kick her feet against the bottom of Emmy's mattress from her bunk below. "I can smell you breathing up there."

Emmy planted herself in front of the coffee table and riffled through the magazines and pamphlets, the scattering of playing cards and odd sections of old newspapers. She touched each thing, then put it back down again. The playing cards had been Linus's. The deck was not full—she counted only fifty cards—but when she lifted her hand to toss them into the trash sack, she hesitated. She couldn't waste them that way. Beside the cards, she found an unredeemed pizza coupon, a Xeroxed copy of an article she meant to read later, an advertisement for a carpet cleaning service she thought she still might try. She shuffled through the mess, sorted it into neater piles without discarding anything, and moved on to the bookcase.

Most of the living room furniture belonged to Linus. The white sectional was his, something he had bought right out of college, the day he got his first job, because he could afford it. "I don't even think I really care for it," he'd said once. "I mean, white. White! What was I thinking, buying a white corduroy couch?" He'd thrown his hands up near his face, a habit that bothered her, made him seem effeminate, flighty. But when they broke up, and he moved into a studio in a downtown neighborhood, he asked if she would keep it for him, store it until he found a better place and could take it back.

The brass floor lamps were his as well, and the heavy iron end table with its thick glass top. Emmy moved between the hulking figures of these things, eyeing them, running her palm along the surface of the bookshelves and the TV to collect dust. She straightened the throw pillows on the couch, adjusted the angle of the reading lamp on the desk in the corner, spent an hour rearranging the books on the shelves, separating novels from science fiction, old college texts from self-help guides. She couldn't throw any of it away.

Upstairs in the bedroom it was the same story. She dragged her plastic sack into the closet and stood before the row of clothes. There were rain slickers and parkas, a ski jacket she had only worn once, and three prom dresses—two of them Ava's. The wire hangers were bent and jammed close together on the rack, a few outgrown skirts and an old pair of size twelve slacks Emmy no longer fit heaped on the floor below, on top of the shoes. Emmy opened her bag and selected a plaid shirt that had been Linus's. She lifted the sleeve to her face, breathed the strong scent of his sweat, tangy and cloistered, still in the fabric. At the end, before he left, the smell of him in their sheets, in the towels on the bathroom rack, and on his soiled laundry in the hamper had seemed too much for her. She'd carried his laundry to the washer breathing through her mouth, climbed beneath the layers of bedding beside him at night holding her own last gulp of air high in her throat. Emmy wadded the shirt into a ball, dropped it into the bag, and tied a knot in the plastic.

At noon she took a break from her cleaning and stepped out onto the back patio with a cup of hot cocoa and marshmallows. Her feet were bare, and the snow felt good on the thick skin of her heels, frigid and startling. She thought about running out into it, around the apartment and into the street, making pocks in the smooth snow and enjoying the destruction. She imagined heaving herself down, arms and legs spread wide, to imprint the imperfect angel of her body on the back lawn, on the patch of ground beneath the Japanese maple near the driveway, up and down the squat cul de sac out front in a pretty, wrecked pattern. She finished her cocoa and carried the cup back inside, climbed the staircase to start in on the bathroom.

Later in the week Ava called her at work. Emmy had already been to the hospital for her daily visit, and had dropped off dahlias, yellow and fat stemmed, to replace the wasting peonies. Generally, she would have thrown the old flowers out, but she thought the petals might make a good potpourri, and so she'd carried them back to work with her in an empty tissue box and spread them out on her desktop. She worked her fingers along the rows of petals as she listened to Ava, turning them over for an even dry.

"Dr. Jean has given me an assignment," Ava said. It always seemed ridiculous to Emmy, the way the patients referred to him by first name, as if he were a radio shrink, a small-town advice columnist. The name itself bothered her too. When he'd asked her to come in for a family session at the beginning of Ava's stay, she'd introduced herself and called him *Gene*. "No, no no," he laughed. "It's *Jahn*. Like in the book *Les Misérables*. Like *Jean Valjean*." She flushed and apologized, sat down in her seat beside Ava's and ground her back teeth until they tasted hot. She imagined he'd changed the spelling of his given name, thinking himself in need of something more suited to his profession, more messianic.

"I need you to take me to a restaurant," Ava said. "As a test before I'm released. Dr. Jean wants me to prove to myself that I can do it, eat on my own, normally." She stopped. "So will you?"

Emmy straightened the rows of petals, nudged them into order with the nail of her thumb. She liked to stay out of Ava's therapy. Over the years, several of the counselors had asked her to come along for a visit, to take an active role in her sister's recovery. But the sessions felt contrived to Emmy, the concentrated, trained understanding of the therapist, the itchy silences when questions were directed at her. Dr. Jean had blue eyes, the color, she had thought when she first met him, of glacial ice, thick and blue and unmoved. He focused them on her each time she spoke, and she felt the pink in her face rise, the wet prickle of sweat blooming between her shoulder blades, beneath the wide band of her underwear. He never blinked, she'd watched.

"I don't know that I'm the right person for this, Ava," Emmy began. She picked out the browner of the petals, nudged them into a separate pile. "I don't know any good restaurants in town, and I might ruin it for you. I might make you uncomfortable."

It had come out, in one of the therapy sessions, that Ava couldn't stand watching other people eat. That as a child she'd watched her family across the dinner table every night, disgusted. They didn't cut their food into small enough pieces. They opened their mouths too wide around each bite, like animals—horses or cows. And Emmy in particular hummed sometimes, if she liked the meal. It had made Ava self-conscious about eating in front of others herself, wondering if she looked the same way. As if, Emmy remembered the words exactly, "she were chewing her cud."

"Emmy," Ava said. Emmy could hear the muffled voices of other patients in the hallway, of the hospital intercom system repeating a doctor's name. "I don't have anyone else. I need you to take me."

"All right," Emmy said. She reached for her purse and unzipped it, swept the petals inside.

Later, at home, Emmy took the petals from her purse and carried them in the cup of her palms up the stairs. In the bathroom she waited for the tub to fill, then opened her hands over the water. The petals fluttered to the surface. They floated or sank slowly, a spotting of pink in the center of the bath. She dipped her hand in, stirred. The petals were browned and curling at their edges, creased with bruises from where her purse or her hands had squeezed them.

Emmy took off her clothes and stepped into the tub, sat down. She had imagined the petals would scent the bath, color it slightly pink, like the toilet water in the pretty glass bottle she remembered from her grandmother's medicine cabinet. But when she breathed in, she could smell only the usual mineral scent and soap.

She slipped her body lower, submerging her shoulders, letting petals drift into and out of her open mouth as she sank, closing her eyes and listening to the blanket quiet of water closing her ears.

After Linus left, she had often wondered what would happen if she fell asleep in the tub and sank this way, if she slipped in the shower one morning, or tumbled down the narrow staircase to the landing below. How long until someone would find her? How long until someone missed her and thought to look?

"You don't think I would look?" Ava had said, when Emmy mentioned it. She leaned forward, laid her hand on Emmy's arm. "I'd look for you if you say you'd look for me." She smiled, pinched the skin of Emmy's forearm. "Joking. Of course I'd look for you," she said, and bent to kiss the welt she'd left. "We'll keep each other from disappearing."

When Emmy arrived at the hospital to pick her up for the dinner, Ava had pinned herself into a black cocktail dress. The pins were hidden in deep tucks of fabric that pulled the dress close to Ava's body, showed off the structure of her hipbones. But she couldn't pin the shoulders, and they hung from her frame, sloppy, making her look as if she were a child playing dress-up.

"Let's go," Ava said. She smiled, picked up a beaded handbag one of the other patients had lent her. "I'm famished."

The restaurant Ava had chosen for the evening was downtown near the piers, on the top floor of a windowed building that looked out over the city and Puget Sound. The ceiling was draped with white sheeting that billowed and drifted down the walls, and rather than chairs, there was a plush white seat around each table, upholstered in velvet or chintz or chenille. Gardenia blossoms and white candles floated in bowls of water that served as centerpieces, taper candles flickered overhead from the low-hung chandeliers. Ava slid into her place behind the table and sat upright, stiff, with her shoulders back and her hands folded on the tabletop beside her napkin. She looked stark in the black dress, in the midst of so much white. She looked fragile as a straight pin.

Emmy opened her menu. She would not order soup, she had decided before coming, or anything with spinach. The one would make her slurp, and the other could be messy. She scanned the menu for something solid, something without crumbs or lumps or seeds that might stick themselves between her teeth and disgust her sister when she opened her mouth to speak.

"Do you eat out often?" Ava asked. Her voice was high and formal, and she unfolded her napkin as she spoke, laid it in her lap, and smiled tightly at Emmy without parting her lips.

Emmy closed her menu, decided on the sautéed shrimp and duchess potatoes. "I eat take-out," she said, and reached for her water. The glass was full, and a dribble of water ran down her chin. She picked up her napkin, dabbed at the water. "Sorry," she said.

"When I come to stay with you, we'll get take-out." Ava kept her eyes on the door. "I used to like Chinese, I remember that. And Indian. I can't remember what anything tastes like anymore, so we'll have to order them both, see if I still like them. Which do you like best?" Ava moved her fingers over the fork and knife, aligning them, inching them parallel to the plate.

Emmy looked at her own place setting. She had flung the silverware from the napkin when the water spilled, and the fork lay across the knife with its tines down, as if about to stab into the table. "I don't know. Linus and I used to order every Friday from a Thai place on Ninety-sixth," she said, and righted her silverware in front of her. "I guess I like Thai."

"Linus," Ava rolled her eyes without taking them from the door. There was regret in her voice, perhaps on Emmy's behalf, perhaps only because the mention of him had intruded on her evening.

"Yes," Emmy said. "He liked Thai food, and I do too."

"Of course you do," Ava said. She looked at Emmy a moment, then away. "Dr. Jean was right about you." Ava sat back against the white fabric of the booth and crossed her arms over her body. "After you left the last time, we talked about you. He said you and I have the same problem in some ways."

The noise of the restaurant around them seemed to float in the room, drift among the white drapery and cushions, and then absorb. Emmy listened to the muffled clamor, as if the whole place were submerged in shallow water. "What?" she said.

But the waiter had arrived and was writing down Ava's order. "Green salad," Ava said, but she hadn't considered the dressing, and she held her menu open wide in front of her face as the waiter listed the available dressings once and then again, more slowly, as if Ava's hearing were her problem. He smiled, kind, and leaned forward toward her so that she pushed herself back against the white booth and drew the menu closer to her chest, looked wildly at Emmy.

One spring—the spring they toured Italy—they ate every dinner at a different restaurant Ava selected. They made dinner an event, returning to their hotel room in the late afternoon so they would have time to shower and let their hair dry before going out, slipping on starched cotton dresses and sandals they had bought together, just the same, with flat soles and leather thongs that laced up their calves like dancers' ribbons. Ava always ordered for them then—she was older. Wine and bread first, then more wine and dinner—a shrimp diavolo or veal scallopini or piccata with saffron rice—then more wine again until they unlaced their sandals and walked back to the hotel barefoot sometimes, stupidly, in the dark streets they did not know.

"Don't you feel different here?" Ava had asked one night. The sun was just down, the street lamps not yet on, and the air smelled wet and muddy like rain coming. Ava held her sandals in her hand and swayed as she walked, so that the only noise in the empty street was the brushed sound of her skirt, its fabric gathering and ungathering around her knees as she moved. "I want to live this way every day," she said. "Like someone else's life. Like I've disappeared inside it."

Emmy closed her menu. "My sister will have vinaigrette," she said, "on the side, please. And a roll, no butter." She did not look at Ava as she gave the waiter her own order, but beneath the table she felt Ava's hand on her knee, cold, thankful.

After dinner Ava wanted to walk awhile, and so they followed the piers along the waterfront. From the restaurant windows, the city had looked thick, a fat cluster of light spread out below the building. But from the street it was darker. The last trace of snow along the roadway was dirty and crystallized and wasting. Most of the tourist shops had closed for the night, turned off their neon window signs, and pulled the metal grates down over their doors. Only the windows at the aquarium were lit, the black, glossy bodies of fish sliding in and out of sight behind the glass. As they walked, there was the sound of water beneath their feet, of waves lumbering in and moving against the wooden pilings of the pier, the dark smell of the water soaked into the wooden planks, into the air, into their hair and coats.

Ava stopped in front of the market at the end of the street. During the day the sidewalk would be crowded with five-gallon buckets of daffodils and tulips, baby's breath, and small, garden-grown roses. But all of the buckets had been dragged inside or carried off in the backs of vendors' trucks for the night, and the sidewalk was bare. "Tomorrow's Monday," Ava said. She was wrapped in her own coat and Emmy's scarf and hat, the black hem of her dress hanging awkwardly from beneath the coat, the black lace of her slip just showing above her knees. "Will you come at lunch time?"

Emmy turned to start back toward the car. She was thinking of home, of sliding into the bath, where the salt smell of the evening would be washed away as she lay on her back, weightless for a few moments at least, in the warm water. She looked to her sister. "Of course," she said. She held out her hand for Ava to take, and they walked holding on to one another in the dark.

A Visitor

The girl stood on the other side of the screen door when March answered the knock. She looked different, smaller, of course, but her hair had grown, and the way it hung down long and uncombed made her look even younger than she had before. She did not take her hands from the pockets of her sweatshirt, but stared at March through the mesh of the screen door. "I'd like to see the baby," she said.

Beyond the door, the sidewalk and street were wet and slick from the earlier rain, the gutters still gurgling with water, but the bay farther off was still.

March opened the door, and the girl stepped inside. Her face was wide and round and unmade-up, and March wondered if she could be called pretty. The girl brought the silvered smell of outdoor air in on her body.

"Did you walk here?" March said. She didn't sit. She hadn't closed the front door but stood next to it, her hand on the knob as if the girl might not stay long, might get up in the next second and leave again and then March could close and lock the door behind her.

But the girl sat down on the couch, pushed herself back against the pillows. "I remembered your address from the papers," she said. "I wondered if you'd be by the water, but I didn't guess so close. You have a view." Her eyes drifted around the room slowly. The furniture was new, March and Peter's Christmas gift to themselves last year. It was meant to look expensive and modern. Peter wanted dark brown leather, and March liked soft couches, wide bookshelves. She had added ceramic vases here and there, stacks of books on the end tables. She kept the bowl on the coffee table full of fat oranges. "You have nice things," the girl said. "This is a nice place for her."

"We're still paying for the house," March said. "Trying to save." She shifted her weight from foot to foot. On the other side of the screen door the bay was flat and dark and glassy, the sky milky and gray as soapy bath water. March had carried Jana out for a walk along the shoreline earlier, and they had found the body of a crow, one wing broken and cocked at a peculiar angle, the black feathers of its body wet, shining. When Jana reached out for it, March had slapped her little hand.

"I don't mean to bother you," the girl finally raised her eyes to meet March's. "I just wanted to see the baby."

"Jana," March said the baby's name. She took in a breath and closed the door.

The girl leaned forward toward the coffee table where an album of baby pictures was stacked on top of a pile of magazines. "Tomorrow is her birthday."

March stepped toward the kitchen. "I'm going to get a drink." She paused. "Do you drink tea?"

The girl had the album on her lap, her hair spilled over her face, and she didn't answer.

In the kitchen March put water on the stove and filled the bottom of a mug with rum before dropping in a tea bag. She spooned sugar into another mug for the girl. It had been a year since they'd last seen her. A letter had come in July, while they had Jana away at Peter's parents' house. Inside the letter the girl had tucked a school photograph of herself and another boy—not Jana's father—at a spring dance. An arch of silk flowers framed the two of them, the boy grinning in an oversized tux, and the girl, still round where Jana had been all those months, standing stiff beside him in a blue satin dress. On the back the girl had written, *Jimmy and Kay, Junior Formal*, and underneath that had drawn a chubby, buoyant-looking heart. March had thrown both the letter and photograph into the wastebasket with the rest of the junk mail.

She couldn't help but notice now, seeing the girl again in person, how much Jana resembled her. Around the eyes and the nose, Jana was an exact copy of the girl. She would never have March's fair coloring or Peter's red hair.

When the water boiled March filled the mugs and took them to the front room.

"Is she walking now?" the girl asked. She looked up from the album and took the tea. "I'd like to see her walk."

"She's on an errand with her father," March said. But then, "She started walking in September. She almost runs now, especially when Peter comes home from work, or to catch our neighbors' dog. She likes dogs. We may get her one this year." March felt the warm ache of the rum ease its way down her throat, fingering out in her chest and stomach, a burn and then a numbing.

The girl had first come to March and Peter through the agency. One afternoon in October the agency called: they finally had a girl who might be right, they said, who would deliver in January. March remembered the day of the call now as an anniversary of sorts, and had bought champagne on the date this October. "To celebrate the day our life changed," she said to Peter.

The agency was Catholic, a group of nuns and laywomen who had started out of a parish across town. "Chosen Ones," they called the adoption service. Most of the girls who came to them were the daughters of parishioners.

"Isn't that funny," Peter had said, and laughed. "Chosen or Fallen?"

There were photographs on the wall of all the babies the Sisters had delivered into the arms of adoptive parents— rosy-cheeked, fat-faced cherubs and beaming, stunned-looking couples. March had reached over for Peter's hand as they sat down, held it in her own two until he took it back when the Sister began to talk about the child who could be theirs. The Sisters talked about adoption that way, like predestination. Like part of the plan. Before March and Peter left the office, Sister Marguerite folded her hands on top of her desk, said, "Let's pray about this."

Peter looked at March as the Sister bowed her head, his face set and hard.

"What's the difference if you don't believe it?" March asked later as they drove home. "What's the difference to you, if it makes us the right kind of parents?"

Peter leaned forward and turned up the volume on the radio so that the window beside March's ear vibrated against its frame, and the sound tremored in her center.

March took her tea to the corner of the living room and sat down in Peter's tall-backed chair near the window. Out on the lawn Jana's plastic beach ball sagged, deflated, and next to the fence her blue plastic pool hadn't been moved since summer. Around it a circle of brown was creeping across the grass, and the water inside the pool was clotted with fallen leaves.

The girl paged through the album of family pictures slowly, her fingers leaving sweaty prints on the plastic page jackets. "I've wondered what she looks like. You know, if she has hair yet, or any teeth. She's chubby like I was," the girl said. "She'll grow out of it, though. You can tell her that."

"Peter's mother says Jana walks like he did as a baby," March said. She held her mug of tea between her two hands. "She does I think. She takes after him."

The girl looked up from the album. "You're taking good care of her," she said. Her eyes were pale and wide and limpid. "Just like she was really yours."

The Sister had said the girl was young—only a junior at the high school—and she couldn't keep the baby. She lived with her mother and stepfather not far from March and Peter. She had fair grades, and until the pregnancy, she had worked at the mall after school. She had signed a form stating that she hadn't had a drink or a cigarette since the baby's conception. She didn't use drugs. She didn't have AIDS. As far as the girl knew, there were no genetic diseases in her family or her boyfriend's. No history of diabetes or cancer or psychiatric abnormalities. No birth defects. No learning disorders. And the baby would be a girl.

"We should meet her," Peter said later, at home. "We should see what she looks like, how she talks to us. Those things they told us, about how healthy she is, how careful with her baby, those could all be lies."

March sat at the dressing table in the bedroom, swirling blush onto her cheeks. She wanted only to go out to dinner, to be in an unfamiliar restaurant with its impersonal chiming of silverware and the blur of other people's conversations filling up the room. She wished to be anywhere but in the house, which felt small and claustrophobic and empty all at once.

Peter put his hands on her shoulders, rubbed his thumbs down into the muscle hard. "They might be the Church," he said, "but they're in the business of getting rid of babies, March."

She looked away from his eyes in the mirror, shifted so that he dropped his hands from her shoulders.

The first year they were together, he'd taken her to meet his parents. Their house was squat and yellow, with a wide porch and a yard surrounded by a short stone wall Peter and his father built by setting river rocks into concrete. "I've lifted every one of those rocks," Peter said. "That's the summer after tenth grade right there."

Peter's mother was warm, round. She had baked Christmas cookies and pies, presented a rump roast or a glazed turkey each night for dinner, so that March worried about overstuffing herself, looking to Peter like she'd lost all self-control. Her own mother had never cooked, never baked a batch of Christmas cookies. But when she said as much, Peter's mother laughed and swatted at March's hand with her napkin. "Eat! Eat!" she said. "There's always enough in this house."

All three of them had red hair, red like March had never seen before, pale and not orange. A thin, nearly pinkish red, and skin that flushed with cold or joy or anger. March had wondered then if Peter's children would be redheads, if they would inherit their father's complexion or her own. If they would inherit his stoic temperament.

"I want to call the Sister back in the morning and sign the papers tomorrow," March said, pulling on her long, black dress. She motioned to her back. "The zip," she said, pressing her palms along the line of the fabric, straightening it. She turned to face him.

Peter didn't say anything but moved toward her in a way that made March step back suddenly, hitting her head against the wall. Her mouth opened and closed, and she reached up, felt for blood and found none.

The light outside the window was beginning to fail, and the corners of the room were already in shadow, the bed still unmade because March had been in such a rush to get to the agency that morning.

She went to the bed and sat down.

"You can't always control things, March," Peter said, his voice even and still. He fisted and opened his hands, fisted and opened them, then walked to the bed to sit beside her. "Let me help you," he said. He touched her so that she turned and offered her back to him, let him zipper the dress. "I don't understand why you can't just be happy," he said. "Why this can't just be enough."

March was quiet. A tender, hard lump was already rising on the back of her scalp, and ached.

For days after, she found herself raising a hand to her head, touching carefully at the bruise to see if it had gone.

In the living room the girl closed the album and sat back against the couch. March had her eyes on the window. The rain had begun again and the girl would have to walk home in it. "I had four miscarriages before Jana," March said. "I don't think you knew that."

The girl picked up her tea and sipped at it for the first time. It had stopped steaming, and March guessed that it would be cold now, the sugar thick and all at the bottom. "I wanted to miscarry," the girl said. "I was praying for it." She looked at March. "But you reminded me of Sarah. You know that Bible story?"

March remembered pieces, though she hadn't heard the story since childhood. An old woman—elderly, ancient. The wrinkles and the gray hair. The husband punished into silence by God.

"When we met you, you reminded me of her, the way you looked at me, I guess. Like you'd rather be sixteen and pregnant than be you." The girl's face flushed. "That didn't come out right," she said.

"No," March said. "I understand."

When they met the girl for the second time, her parents came. They had driven the boy in their car because his own parents didn't know about the baby and wouldn't be told. "I'm going to college next year," the boy said. He had a desperate face, pimpled still and wide-eyed. He looked at the girl as if she were dangerous, the one who had done this to him. When her stepfather reached in his direction for a pen, the boy flinched.

They signed the papers that day, all of them. Peter picked up the pen, then put it down again and looked to the Sister. "Once this is signed, nothing changes, is that right? No one will be at my door in six months wanting the baby back?" The Sister had already explained the girl's rights—the state law that said she had only forty-eight hours once the papers were signed. After that, she could not change her mind.

The girl had her hands folded on the mound of her belly. She kept her eyes on the table. "I promise you that I won't want it back."

"You promise that," March said. She had been quiet at the table until then, and when she spoke her voice was hard, a demand.

The girl looked up and met March's eyes. "I said I promise."

Beyond the front window, the rain picked up. It puckered the smooth surface of the bay.

"I know you wanted to be there," the girl said. "At her birth."

March had wanted to be at the birth. "The hospital will call you," the Sister from the agency said over the phone, "but you can't come into the delivery room. The birth mother has asked that you not be there."

"Why can't we be there?" March stormed later. She had spent the day painting the room that would be Jana's nursery. Frenzied, finishing all the walls in just a few hours, she then drove out to the store to buy diapers and formula and four brown-nippled plastic bottles that she scrubbed at over the sink as she spoke. "Why would she do that to us?"

It was the one time she wanted Peter to yell, to pick up the ceramic vase on the table and throw it, to break things on her behalf. But he sat quiet in his chair at the table, his arms crossed over his chest, watching her. "This is what I said was coming, March," he finally said. He kept his voice unbearably level. "You knew this was coming."

Now the girl shifted on the couch. "I knew you wanted to be there," she repeated, "but I couldn't." She smiled. "Wasn't she so small that day? I only held her that once, right away, before you came to get her, and she was just so small."

When the nurse had come out with Jana, wrapped and new, she'd looked tiny, so much smaller than March had imagined. "Well," the nurse smiled when March said as much, "her birth mother is a small girl."

Across the living room the girl said again, "I knew you wanted to be there. I didn't care."

"It was fine," March said. "We got to see her soon enough." She looked at the girl on her couch. *Birth mother*, she repeated to herself. Only together were they one whole mother.

There was the sound of a car outside the house, and March stood up, watched as it passed. "It's not them," she said. "I don't know when they're coming home. It could be late."

"I thought about this all the time after I met you," the girl said. "You and your house and how she would live." She watched March sit down again but did not move. "The last couple of months before she was born I thought about you all the time. I imagined you when I couldn't sleep."

March nodded. She hadn't slept well during those months either. Beside her, Peter snored quietly, and she tried to follow the in and out of his breath herself, to let his sleep pull her into her own. She listened to the soft sound the rain made on the roof, the oceanic hushing of wind in the leaves of the tree beyond the window. But she could not sleep. She wondered if it was possible to ache with a baby she wasn't carrying. She got up and rubbed her legs where they were sore, dug the heels of her hands into her lower back. Her breasts and her hips felt heavy. Her body felt soft.

The girl set her mug down on the table and stood up. Her eyes moved across the room again and then settled at the window, where she went to stand. She put her hands on the backs of her hips so that her slim body bent forward, as if she'd been listening to March's memories. She said, "You know, I dream sometimes that I've lost her. Misplaced her, I mean, and that I'm looking for her. I dump out the hamper. I look behind the drapery and expect to find her hiding there. And then sometimes I run out into the street to start calling her, but I can't remember her name."

Outside, the line of daylight was slipping into the bay. The sky was ashy and weighted over the flat surface of the water. The yard and the sidewalk beyond it were shadowed with evening.

March hadn't turned any lights on in the house, and the gray darkness that filled the living room felt too close. She fumbled to turn on the lamp beside her, then stood up and went to the girl. When she reached out, the tips of her fingers touched the girl's shoulder. "I'll show you her room," she said. "If you want to see it before you go."

Upstairs March led the girl into the nursery. The lamp was on and glowing on the bureau, its light rosy on the yellow walls. The room had the soft smell of Jana, and the girl sat down in the rocker.

"Peter bought that," March said. "Once we finally had her. He came bringing that home one night. I sit with her there, when she cries at night, and I sing to her."

"My mother used to sing hymns when I couldn't sleep," the girl said. She moved her feet up and down against the floor to rock the chair slowly. "I remember the words still. Do you sing her hymns?"

"Peter reads when he's with her," March said. "Articles from his business magazines, or novels."

"Maybe you could sing a Christmas song, if you don't know any hymns," the girl said. "My mother sang 'Silent Night' sometimes. Maybe you could sing that."

"Maybe," March said.

The girl got up from the chair and took a small, wrapped box from her pocket. "I have a birthday gift for her. You don't have to tell her it's from me, but I'd like her to have it anyway."

It was dark outside, and raining again, a short, hard burst of drops as if the sky just above the house had split open.

"It's not anything she'll like." The girl held the box out toward March. "It's a lace bonnet, for a christening, from my christening. I was saving it." The girl shifted her weight from one foot to the other. "But I think you should keep it, you know, for someday, when she's a little older."

March took the gift.

Tomorrow friends would come for the party she had planned—Peter's sister and parents, a couple of people from his office, and the mother and little girl from down the street. March had ordered cakes a month early, one for the party and a smaller one just for Jana. They would take a picture of her with frosting all over her face, like the picture Peter's mother had of his first birthday. March was making a special lunch of roast and salad, homemade bread that Peter's mother would bake and bring. And there was a doll for Jana hidden away in the closet, wrapped in pink paper and ribboned.

March didn't say anything about the party. She tucked the girl's gift into her own pocket. "I should drive you home," she said, but neither of them moved to go.

"I'm going to college next year," the girl said. Her voice seemed loud in the small room. Her hands were lost again inside the long cuffs of her sweatshirt sleeves. "I might not go here. I might not stay near home. I'm supposed to decide in the next few months if I want to leave or not." She looked to March.

There was the sound of the rain on the roof above their heads and at the window, like a string of beads come undone over a marble floor. In the low, yellowed light of the room, the girl's face looked younger than it had before, and already beaten. The shadows darkened the skin beneath her eyes like soft bruises.

March felt the girl's gift inside her pocket, pressing against her hip. Peter would be home soon. She would see the wet flash of his headlights at the window, hear the rattling of his keys on the unlit front stoop outside, and then his voice in the hallway, coming up to find her.

In his arms though, Jana would be warm and sleepy, radiating her infant smell of baby powder and sweetened milk and new skin. Jana would reach out as soon as she saw her.

March looked toward the wet window. The room was reflected on its glass like another full room she could walk into: Jana's things, softened in the reflection because of the rain, and her own image there against the darkness, and the girl, standing near her.

"We should go downstairs now," March said. She was aware of a certain loosening in her body, and then a kind of tender ache in the muscles of her abdomen and back. She moved to the door and opened it, turning to the girl. "They'll be home soon and we haven't turned on the porch light."

Exhibitions

Marlon was eight when he lost his hand. It was his right hand that he lost, the one he favored. He'd been learning to write smooth letters with it in school. Cursive, he told his mother, but he mispronounced it, the *r* disappearing beneath his slow tongue— *cuw-sive*—the *r* slipping away. He gripped the pencil like a weapon when he wrote, the first two fingers and wide thumb tight, the smallest finger curled into the cup of his palm. Mira watched him at the table with his pencil and paper, his head bent low near the surface while his right hand pressed out the curved, black letters.

"I knew he'd be right-handed," she said to her husband, Eli, as they undressed for bed the night she first saw Marlon write. Eli held a magazine in his hands, turned the pages as Mira folded back the white down comforter that topped the bed, tucked it into neat thirds as she did every night. "All right," she said when she was satisfied with the blankets, and Eli closed the magazine and set it on the floor. They lay down on the mattress leaving a space of sheet between them, their backs rounded toward one another but apart, and both reached to turn out the bed-table lamps. "He was born with a callus there, you remember," she went on. She talked into the darkness of the small bedroom.

"Yes," Eli said now and then from his place beside her, but his breathing began to deepen toward sleep.

"Like a swirl there on that thumb," Mira said. "Sort of hard. White." She pressed her lips together, closed her eyes.

After her son lost his hand, Mira took up growing and researching orchids. She has been growing them nearly twenty years, which she considers quite a feat. It is cold and wet where she lives on Whidbey Island, not orchid weather. The air is gray and soft and porous. Mushrooms sprout between the blades of grass on her lawn and have to be dug up. Pink-black florets of mold blossom along the window ledges in the house and must be bleached dead.

Mira keeps her orchids healthy with heat lamps and spray misters and a careful attention. They are expensive plants, fifty to one hundred dollars each, depending on species and particular beauty. They are fragile and startling and perfectly formed.

When she is not tending her orchids, Mira is researching others on her computer, species she cannot buy even if she takes the ferry to the mainland and drives in to shop the exotic florist stores in Seattle. She types in a name, and a full-color picture appears on the screen in front of her. *Leptotes bicolor,* with its brazen pink center thrusting forward from between white petals. *Articulata,* like a cluster of fingertip-sized stars. And the lovely *magdalenae,* called "Queen of the Angraecums," a thick and droopy-petaled Madagascar orchid, with a spicy scent of far away.

There is satisfaction in just looking at their even forms: the precision of a blossom's balance on its reed-thin stem, the ordered lineup of white buds, the exact flare of a plant's bright petals. Mira could not care for messy flowers—roses or lilies or the unpredictable amaryllis—and she devotes her attention solely to her orchids. In front of her house, she has let the flower beds crowd with weeds and nettles. The blackberries are overgrown and leggy. The rhododendron's sticky red and pink buds have fallen off and are like crumpled litter on her lawn.

Marlon liked to climb things as a boy. Or perhaps it was that he liked to be up high. Mira herself had never even climbed a ladder. Never stood in the high fork of two tree branches and looked out. She was not afraid of heights, but she liked the ground and its certain firmness. On the Fourth of July, when they rode the ferry across the water to Eli's parents' house, everyone else climbed up the rickety old staircase to the flat roof to watch the fireworks while Mira remained on the grass below. She sat on a lawn chair in the darkness alone, her knees pushed tight together to hold the bottle of beer she'd been sipping from all evening, and watched the display with her feet still touching the ground.

"Are you coming up?" Eli always stopped to ask as he passed her on his way to the roof himself. He carried a soda can in his hand and had tucked a blanket beneath his arm. He bent forward and put his lips to her hair.

"No," she said. "I'll stay here." She squeezed her knees against her warm beer bottle.

Eli straightened, shifted the blanket under his elbow. "I wish you wouldn't always," he said. "I wish you'd come up with the rest of us, so you could see it all better. This ruins it, doesn't it? Sitting here?"

He stood near her chair, then finally crossed the lawn, and in a moment she turned when he called to her from the rooftop, his voice thinned by the distance, so that she could only narrowly hear him. "You won't see as much," she thought she heard him say. She raised her hand to wave as if she hadn't heard him, though, turned back around in her chair.

Marlon said he liked to climb because he could see everything from up high. He could see the world from the roof of the shed behind their house: the small square of the neighbors' yard, the next street over, the water and the shore across the Sound. He could see the spot at the end of the block where he turned his bike around before riding back home again. He rode loops and loops on the bike all afternoon until the ferry came in at six and his father's car appeared at the end of the street. Then one last loop before riding home for dinner.

Marlon had a round face Mira couldn't place among the family, but also his father's hairline with the triangle peak in the center, and the same wide forehead that gave them both a look of calm assuredness. His eyes were dark and his eyebrows thick, so that he seemed always to be watching. He smelled the way boys do—like sweet child-sweat and grass and salty mud—but he was Mira's only boy, and so while he slept, she often slipped into the night-light glow of his bedroom and put her face to his hair, kissed the soft skin inside his elbow as she tucked his arm beneath the blankets.

Eli believes he is indulgent about the orchids—he has said this to Mira often over the years, and to other people, whenever the orchids have come up. He doesn't mention the money or the space the orchids consume, and now and then he brings one home as a gift for her, a common lady's slipper or some other hothouse variety. The ones he brings home lean limp, their blossoms wilting, and Mira takes them from him and sets them out in the front room or in the window ledge near the door. They are always white or yellow or flecked with brown, and he brings them to her in grocery store pots still wrapped in cellophane, rubber banded, a white plastic name tag reading only "ORCHID" still dug into the soil beside the stem. They always fail quickly, and Mira carries them out back to the compost pile and shakes loose the clots of dirt and dried roots from their pots, drops the plastic pots into the trash can. "Eli," she says every time he brings one home, but he keeps bringing them, for her *collection*, a word that makes Mira think of ugly hobbies: hoarding porcelain figurines or filing stamps or dangling silver-plated tourist spoons from wooden boxes on the walls. He does not see the difference.

She is bent over one of her orchids with her tweezers and spray mister when he comes up behind her one evening. "Looks good," he says. He reaches forward and touches one of the pink petals in a way that makes her draw in her breath, then takes his hand away. "Pretty." She feels his chest against her back, the press of him. "Are you coming up to bed soon?" he asks. "It's late."

Mira thinks, *Go*. But she turns around and lets him kiss her. The tweezers and mister still in her hands, she holds her arms away from him, in the air, while he embraces her. "Have you brushed your teeth yet?" she asks as she pulls away. She turns her back to him. "I'm still working," she says. She listens until she hears him leave her, the silence refilling the space he has left, like water closing in.

The day Marlon lost his hand is still and drained of its color in Mira's mind, like the old kind of photograph, the image stopped by a blast of white light. Her eyes hurt when she remembers. The sun had been bright all that day, unexpectedly, and she'd stayed inside. She didn't hear him scream, and when she thought to look for him through the kitchen window, she saw him lying on the grass beneath the shed. She thought of broken branches then, in the woods near the house where she was raised. She thought of walking through the trees as a little girl, snapping twigs between her hands. There was always a crack when a branch finally gave, and the tremor of pleasure she felt in breaking it.

When she touched her son, Marlon's eyes were wide and animal.

"I wanted to fly," Marlon told the doctor later. He had jumped off the roof of the shed. If he had simply fallen, his wrist might have been sprained, but instead he'd gotten scared and tried to stop himself, and he had caught his hand on the ragged blade-edge of the roof. The hand was useless. All of the ligaments and tendons had been torn up in the moment the boy had hung there before falling, and were severed entirely when he finally fell. How long had he lain there on the grass? Mira wasn't sure. She wasn't sure why she hadn't heard him falling.

The wound had bled through Marlon's shirt, soaked a mud-colored stain onto the fabric. When the doctor pulled it from his body, Mira stepped away. The blood was a cracked scab on Marlon's chest, a reptilian second skin.

At home, Mira washed her son carefully, filling the bathtub with water she tested by dipping in an elbow. She was afraid her boy would slip climbing in—he couldn't brace himself with his hands as he sat down into the water anymore—so she held him like an infant and set him into the tub. He raised the wrapped arm, a mitten of hospital gauze and bandaging over the wound where his hand had been. He held it up close to her face and wiggled it. "Hi, Mama." The boy made his voice high and squeaky. "Hi, Mama." He wiggled the arm at her and laughed.

Nearly every weekend now Mira leaves Eli asleep in the empty house and boards the early ferry to the mainland for an orchid exhibit or a meeting of growers. There are clubs for orchid lovers as well, though she doesn't belong to any. She went to a club meeting once, several years ago, when she first began growing orchids, but the people were bland, just hobbyists, and she was the youngest person in the room by several years. The rest of them were elderly. They smelled of ointment and of wool, a scent that reminded her somehow of her mother's preserves, shrunken apricots pressed against the glass of Mason jars. She couldn't bear listening to them go on and on about their wilted orchids. She left the meeting early.

The exhibitions are not so amateur. Growers drive from as far away as Boise and Sacramento, their orchids tented beneath tight, dewy bubbles of plastic in their cars. She wanders among the set-up booths and displays, leans in close to examine new species, and in her mind compares what she has at home to what these others have brought. Weak stems, she thinks. Brown-rimmed petals and lazy buds. She feels the satisfied sheen of perfection glinting inside herself when she considers her own well-kept plants. Walking the long rows of orchid booths, Mira is something close to content.

At school, after the accident, Marlon learned to use his left hand. He wrote crooked, wobbly letters that his mother pinned to the refrigerator beside the picture of him that she kept there, a picture of him holding a fishing pole in his left hand, a fish in his right. The right hand in the picture looked white and strong. It wasn't a good photograph, but she kept it up because it was the last picture of him before the accident. It was the last photograph in which nothing was wrong about her boy.

Marlon himself seemed not to mind his disability. He was not self-pitying, not overly determined. He seemed not to notice his own awkward fumblings. For the first couple of months, he occasionally missed his mouth when eating with his left hand. Mira watched him from her place at the table. He held the fork like a spear. Although her husband got up when he finished his own dinner, pushed back his chair and left his napkin dangling off the edge of the table, Mira waited for her son. She inched her empty plate away from herself and put her elbows on the table, rested her chin on her hands while Marlon stabbed and shoveled. She watched him open his mouth for the fork the way a young bird waits for its food. In the other room, Eli shuffled the newspaper, turned on the television set. When he finished, Marlon stood up, dropped his napkin on the table just as his father had, and left her.

That and other things stayed in Mira's mind, made her want to lean toward the boy when he stood beside her, to scoop him up or stand behind him and offer her own right hand in place of his own. When she saw other children, hands and feet fingered and toed precisely, she hated them softly. She wanted to reach out and slap each little face red.

In the spring, Mira enters one of her orchids in a contest. It is ready, she thinks. The arch of its stem reminds her of the arches of dancers' backs as they bend and sway across a stage: precisely trained. The blossoms on the plant are white and wide, like the pretty, flat faces of lionesses. They float on air.

As he grew, Marlon began to look more and more like his father. The easy, slow kinesis of his body, how he moved his mouth around his words when he spoke, the myopic way he could sweep his eyes around a room and see everything without seeing anything really.

In high school Marlon bought his first camera. He couldn't play tennis or baseball after school like the other boys, and instead interned himself to the local paper. He liked to practice taking photographs out in the yard after dinner and developed a rhythm with the camera that Mira could hear from inside the house. The mechanical shutter swoosh, back-and-forth, snap. And then, like lightning, the blue-white of his flash illumined the yard, his face, his hand holding the camera. He perfected a precarious balance, the camera perched like a black bird on his right forearm and resting there securely. He is a contortionist, she thought, watching him through the kitchen window, the way he moved his left hand over his own head, arced the angle of his elbow to keep his arm from the picture's frame as he snapped the shutter. Back-and-forth, snap. The lopsided sound, the following silence.

In the mornings he left the house early. She would hear him moving about the kitchen and would get up, drink a cup of coffee at the kitchen table while he finished his breakfast of a glass of milk and an orange. He sat across from her and peeled the orange slowly with his left hand, poking his thumbnail in deep at the navel and running it just beneath the skin. As he ate the first section, he wound the orange curl of peel back into a whole and held it up for her. "Voilà," he said. Every morning he said it. When he left, he kissed the top of her head and swung his camera strap over his neck, picked up the pack that held his lenses and his film.

Marlon took photographs of nothing: children playing on the lawn in front of the City Hall; a dog grinning beside the newly painted red fire hydrants on Center Street; passengers unloading from the ferry. He was given assignments that the men at the newspaper office were sure he could handle. "Mother," he said, unbothered. "I'm new. What else could be expected?"

Mira thought about how hard she would have to slap a

full-grown newspaper editor to leave the mark of her hand on his cheek.

But she saw that the editors were right, that he was not ready for more, that his photographs were obvious in their imperfection, even to her untrained eyes. "Marlon," she would say appreciatively when he handed her a new photograph of boats docked in the harbor or children playing ball at the park. "You've captured just how this looks." And while she said it, she spotted the misplacement of a certain cloud in the marbled sky, the way a sail hung slack and dingy from its mast in the foreground of the photo. "Good," she said, and smiled, handing it back to him without mentioning the error of his sight.

Sometimes, when Mira washed the clothes, she held her son's shirts to her face, trying to remember the way he'd once smelled—that grassy scent of a boy—then further back, to new skin and her own milk. Her laundry room had grown the smell of men, wet and green, and a little bit feral. She piled her son's clothes into a heap, washed and hung them out on the line she had strung across the laundry room, though she had an electric dryer. On the line the clothes dried evenly and without wrinkles. When the sun fell in through the window, their shadows drew definite outlines of Marlon's body on the wall.

Mira lets Eli come with her to the contest. He carries her purse and a sack lunch she has packed for them. They board the first ferry and find seats at a booth on the first deck, where it is warm and the cafeteria smells of coffee and doughnuts sift out to them.

"Do you want anything?" Eli stands and asks her. He holds his coat over his arm and has tucked a copy of the *Seattle P. I.* under his elbow.

"No. I'm feeling sick already. Nerves," she says. She holds the orchid on her lap carefully. It is trapped inside a plastic dome she created out of sticks and tape and a sheet of thick, clear plastic. She blew warm air from her hair dryer up inside it, bloating the plastic out around the plant, and stuck the nose of the mister in for a quick spritz of water before sealing it all up to trap the heat and moisture inside. She peers in at the plant. It looks fine. She is glad she went to the trouble.

When Eli returns, he sets a cup of coffee in front of her. "One cream, no sugar," he says. "You should have something at least."

"Thank you," she says. "I didn't want anything." She lifts the cup to her mouth and sips. "You'll be bored today. You didn't have to come."

He nods. He has opened up the paper and pulled out the section on local news. He will throw the rest away, as he always does. Normally Mira might say something, mention the wastefulness of spending a dollar on something he's only going to look at one page of, but her stomach is tight and she keeps quiet. "Look," he says from behind the news. He folds the paper back so she can see, and she sits up and cranes her neck a little. "It's one of Marlon's. 'Marlon McMahon,'" he reads. He has his finger on a photograph of tulip fields. Red and yellow stripe the image of a sea of tulips. "It's titled 'April Showers Bring Local Flowers to Glorious Bloom.'" Eli taps his finger on the newspaper and grins. "Nice," he says. He sips his coffee and brings the paper back up to read it. "I wonder if he'll be assigned to your show today. Your contest."

Mira draws in a breath. She hadn't thought the papers would cover the orchid show, but they could. She hadn't thought of it. She pulls the bagged plant closer to her body. It's drafty where she's sitting. People keep opening the doors to the outer deck, letting in wet gusts of saltwater air. "No," she says aloud.

"Sorry?" Eli raises his eyes above the newspaper.

"Nothing," Mira says. "I didn't say anything." She clutches the orchid to her body as another passenger opens the doors to the wind.

Mira went to Marlon's apartment once, just after he moved in. It was a long way for her, the ferry ride first, then the drive south all the way down to Seattle. She rounded his block four times before choosing a parking spot and stopping.

"Mother," Marlon said when he opened his door. He hugged her. She was always aware of the lopsidedness of his hugs, the left hand firm on her shoulder blade, and the rigid brace of the right forearm. He stepped back and smiled at her. "Come in. Sit down. Do you want tea? Or anything?"

She shook her head and sat down on his sofa. The cushions were oversized and pale yellow, an impractical brushed suede that would eventually wear lighter in the spots where people often sat. She sank into it and tried to push herself back up. "This is quite a sofa," she said.

"It's comfortable." Marlon sat down at the opposite end of the sofa and crossed his right leg over his left knee. She had never seen him sit that way before. It made him seem to slouch. She looked at his dark blue pants on the soft yellow fabric of the cushions.

The apartment was clean but full. There was a round coffee table in front of the sofa, and a round kitchen table with four chairs, all in cherry-colored wood, near the kitchen. A bookshelf stood against a wall in the living room, and another sat squat in the corner, stacked with books and file folders, old newspapers and magazines in which Marlon's photographs had appeared. She hadn't known he'd saved these things. She had saved them. She kept them tucked into a metal cabinet in the back den at home, along with his high school diploma, his college bills and grade reports, his medical files.

On every wall four or five bright photographs hung in silver frames. All of them were of birds, though big birds, not sparrows or jays or gulls. Marlon had made trips since college down to California and Utah, Nevada and Wyoming, and the pictures in his apartment were ones he had shot on those trips, of eagles and of cranes, of herons and hawks, all wide-winged and in flight.

"I saw you had something in the news the other day," she said. "A parade?"

"There was a parade downtown. They sent me to get photos of the clowns."

She remembered. The photograph had seemed busy to her, crowded. Heads and heads of people clustered together in the street between the fences of city buildings, the bright mopped wigs of the clowns. She could hardly pick one face out from another, and had folded the paper cleanly and slipped it into the filing cabinet.

"It was nice," she said.

The door opened then, and a young blond woman stepped in, her arms full of grocery sacks and her coat sliding from one shoulder. "Marlon," she called to him as she edged around the door and shut it. Marlon jumped up from the sofa and took the bags from her, balancing the one on his right arm in a way that made Mira stand up.

"Oh no," the girl said. "Don't stand up for me. Please. Sit down." She stepped forward and took Mira's hand in her own cold fingers. "I'm Elaine."

She wore a close-fitting, white turtleneck sweater that showed off how slim she was, how delicate looking. The part in her hair was straight, and her ponytail was long and tight and shining the white-yellow of field grass in October, bleached and nearly colorless. She sat down across from Mira in a wide blue armchair whose cushions seemed to swallow her up before she straightened and crossed her legs at the ankles.

Mira watched her son putting away the groceries in the kitchen. The apartment was all one big room, so she could see him from where she sat without seeming to stare. His movements had become smooth. She remembered the way he had moved after the injury, like a toddler, adding extra steps to every chore awkwardly. But Marlon looked easy now, as if the seams in his movements had smoothed out. Still, Mira wondered, why wasn't the girl helping him?

He finished emptying the grocery sacks and began to slide himself into the chair beside Elaine, then stood up again and leaned against the chair's arm instead. "I'm sorry you had to introduce yourselves," he said. He raised his left hand and brushed a strand of hair from Elaine's face. "I should have brought her home to meet you, but this is just how it worked out."

"I've met your husband, actually," the girl said. She had small white teeth and the kind of smile that showed them, her lip pulling up to reveal a clean line of pink gum. "We went to the island to pick up some of Marlon's things, at your house, and he was there—Eli."

Mira startled when the girl called her husband by his first name, familiarly, as if she were already a part of the family.

"You weren't home that day," Marlon said. "You were at a show."

"I love orchids," the girl spoke over his words, interrupting. "My mother grows them too. She grows lady's slippers that look like tiny Cinderella shoes. Don't you think they look like that? Perfectly like that."

Marlon kissed the top of her head.

Mira wondered how the girl stood it when he touched her. She imagined her son's left hand running down the naked length of this girl's body, or reaching up to smooth her hair. She imagined the girl inside the angle of his right arm, that press, and the way it just dropped off suddenly where the hand had once been but now there was nothing but skin, shiny and round and strange.

That evening, when Mira got home, it was late and dark. Eli was sitting at the kitchen table with a bowl of ice cream. He looked up at her as she came in the front door. "You're home," he said, and he pointed toward the freezer. "There's another bowl in there for you."

Mira dropped her keys onto the counter. "You didn't tell me you'd met Elaine," she said. The girl's name felt like a piece of glass on her tongue.

"Oh." Eli raised his spoon to his mouth. "Elaine. You met her."

"She's talkative," Mira went on. "Marlon just lets her talk and talk." Mira laid her coat over the back of her chair and sat down. She set her elbows on the table, crossed her arms over her chest. "I can't believe," she said. Her voice sounded both small and heavy when she spoke.

"I'd think you of all people would be happy with her," Eli said.

"What?" Mira asked, but Eli spooned the last of the ice cream from his dish to his mouth and got up from the table. Mira watched him rinse the bowl and leave it in the sink. "I was the last to meet her," she said. "The last one."

Eli stood with his back against the countertop, his eyes on the floor or his feet, somewhere other than on Mira. She remembered how he'd ruffled Marlon's hair that night after the fall and the hospital, just ruffled it with his fingers. "All right, buddy?" he'd said. "You going to be all right now?"

"He told you," she said. She had not turned the light on when she'd come into the room earlier, and there was only the artificial blue glow of the orchids' heat lamp in the dark kitchen, the even hum of its burning.

Eli shifted his weight and started for the stairs. "You've got to give him some room, Mira," he said as he left her. "You need to."

Later, she left the bedroom window open when she went to bed, let the drops of rain spit in and seep into the wood ledge. It didn't matter. She could feel Eli's breath on her shoulder, and pulled the blanket up between them. On her back, she closed her eyes and imagined the old sound of her son's camera in the backyard. The back-and-forth, snap. The way the room had lit up around her like an explosion, like a sudden idea. It had looked the way her heart sometimes felt inside her chest, like a white fire.

"Marlon?" she used to say to him when she heard the screen door close at his back.

"Yes. It's me."

And then she could sleep.

At the exhibition hall she looks around but doesn't see Marlon. There is a man with a camera, but he is short, square-bodied, and not from the *P. I.* but from a gardening magazine. She walks to the table displaying the contest orchids and finds her name already written out on a card. She sets her plant on the table and begins the careful unwrapping. In her purse she has brought her tweezers and mister, an extra length of fishing line in case the ride jostled the plant out of its arch and it has to be re-tied to the stick. She steps back on her heel and narrows her eyes at her orchid, leans forward to readjust the pot, and steps back again. It is fine.

Her stomach is queasy and her fingers jittery from the cup of coffee on the ferry. Eli left to wander the exhibition hall as they first came in, and when she looks out into the crowd of so many people, he has disappeared.

She walks the rows of booths and looks over the orchids. Her impression is what it always is at these shows—that, for the most part, the plants for sale are overpriced and less than quality. The lips of their petals are fringed in brown and their blossoms seem too heavy. They lack that quality of weightlessness she expects them to have, as if they could rise at any moment and leave their stems.

As she moves, she looks over the crowd. Several times she thinks she sees her son after all, and she slips between a cluster of women in front of a booth, tucks her face down. But it is just other men with broad shoulders. Other men wearing coats close to the color of the one she bought Marlon two years ago. Would he bring Elaine to something like this? She searches out blond women in the crowd, and there seem to be hundreds of them.

What would she say if she bumped into Marlon and Elaine now anyway? When she'd left his apartment that day, she'd wanted to hold him. She'd stood at the door staring, her body filling the doorjamb, wanting to scoop him into her arms as she once could, but there was still a holding back. She remembered the blood crusted on his skin the day he fell, the red of the bath water. When she found him in the yard, he had vomited on himself; in the shock, he had wet his pants. She gagged trying to pick him up, and turned away then, leaving him there on the lawn to go back inside. In the minutes of waiting for the ambulance, she watched him through the kitchen window. She stayed inside.

The exhibition hall is warm, and she feels suddenly too hot. There is the taste of bile in her mouth from not having eaten all morning, and the underarms of her blouse are clinging to her skin. She moves away from the crowd to an exhibit at the far end of the hall, braces her hands against the table, and leans her weight down a little.

"Are you all right?" The man behind the booth steps forward.

"I'm fine. It's just a little warm in here, I think."

"You could sit." He offers her the chair he's been sitting on behind the table.

"No. Thank you." Mira's face is flushed now, and she looks up at the man. "Why don't you tell me about your orchids," she says. The man is bald, his head shiny with sweat. It *is* warm in here, she thinks, and feels herself begin to calm.

"This is a Birrimense orchid," the man explains. "Originating in Zimbabwe." His tone is educational, like a tape recording one could check out at the public library. "Darwin made these beauties popular." He is smiling now, and Mira looks down at the plant between his hands.

There is one blossom. It is white, but not a white Mira has seen before, a white that seems foreign, not just to orchids, but to everything. It is white like the moon is white, not really white at all, but bluish, and opalesque as the scales of a deepwater fish. Its petals are thick but fragile, sharp like spears instead of rounded.

The man continues talking, saying something about moths and Darwin that she only half hears.

Yes, she thinks, a moth. The blossom seems spare and spread, its petals extended like an opened hand, like wings. Like a moth in the blue light of dusk, batting at the windows or the globe of a porch light. A sort of lovely desperation she hasn't noticed before, anywhere.

"Moths are not at all beautiful," she says aloud, and the man snorts a laugh, stops talking a moment.

"No," he says. "I don't guess that they are."

"But this is exactly the body of a moth," she goes on. A moth stopped, she thinks. Just as it begins to open its wings. Mira reaches forward, touches her finger and thumb to one of the petals, gentle, not to bruise the blossom. "Yes," she says. "Just as it should be." She lets her breath out; she has been holding it too long.

She leaves the man's booth and walks toward the doors of the exhibition hall. She wants to get outside, where the air is not so crowded with other people's breath. A breeze hits her face as she steps out, gusts around the edges of the mirror-windowed building. Mira squints against the sudden shift of light, lifts a hand to shade her eyes. The hem of her coat flutters up at her sides where she stands.

The Virtuoso

Bente was in the orchard when Ari appeared. She hadn't seen him yet, not closely, and as he walked across the street from the house toward her, she noticed the funny lopsidedness of his gait, the way he swung his long left arm and kept the right one tight around his violin case, the same way David carried his. He had fair skin, a red scarf wrapped twice around his skinny neck, and a knitted snow hat pulled down over his ears.

"You're Mrs. Carlson," he said as he stepped over the ditch between the road and the orchard. His legs were as gangly as his arms.

Bente picked up the sack of apples she'd been collecting and turned back toward the tree. "Bente," she said.

"Are you making sauce, Mrs. Carlson?"

"Bente," she said again. "And no. These are pig apples. They're pretty, but bitter, and I doubt good for much." She stretched up to tug an apple from a higher branch, but her fingers just grazed it. "Could you get it?" she asked, and stepped back. She was out of breath with the cold and the exercise of picking the apples, and she wanted the boy to go and leave her. She would rather have just heard his playing, just the sound of him in the studio above the bedroom ceiling. Now, when she lay in bed at night listening, she would have to picture this thin, awkward boy upstairs, David's hand on his shoulder as he played, David's chin set in determined appreciation of him.

"I'm Ari." He dropped the apple into the bag that she opened for him. His voice was deep and unsuited to his lanky body, which was still so adolescent looking, even for a young graduate student.

"I know," Bente said. She looked up at him. "David's genius. David's always looking for a genius." She wanted to embarrass him, to see him flush or squirm.

But he didn't. "I like playing. That's not why I came to study here, though." He shifted the violin case under his arm. "I should go, but I'm glad we got to meet." He made the long step across the ditch to the road, then turned back to her. "The tart apples make the best pies," he said, and started walking.

When Bente got back to the house, David was at the kitchen table with a cup of coffee and a pencil, several pages of sheet music spread out in front of him. She dumped the apples from the sack into a metal bowl on the counter and set them into the sink to wash. "I met your student," she said.

David put down his pencil and looked up at her. "I saw you talking to him when I came down. I invited him to dinner on Saturday."

Bente picked up an apple, moved her fingers over the lumps beneath its skin. They were probably infested, hollow in their centers and mealy. "Oh?" she said.

David had bent back over his music and was writing along the margins of the paper, marking out directions for himself on how to play the piece. She'd looked at his music before, the way he scrawled all over each page in an illegible hand she couldn't decipher. You could try to write more clearly, she'd said once, so I could read it too. David had stared back at her blankly. Why? he'd said.

"Don't go out of your way," he said. "The boy's been eating cafeteria food all autumn." He stood up and shuffled the papers into a pile, tucked the pencil into the pocket of his shirt. He put his hand to the back of her head, ran his palm down the length of her hair.

Bente turned on the faucet, let the water fill up the sink around the apples. She felt his grasp on her upper arms, the slight squeeze before he walked to the door and left again. To the sink she said, "The boy likes pig-apple pie."

It was October when Ari had first begun coming to the house. Bente learned the sound of his heavy steps on the stairs outside the kitchen, climbing up to the studio. He wore the kind of boots day laborers and farmers wear, thick leather with treaded, toothy soles that tracked clots of dry mud and grass inside. Once he left, Bente could always hear the whisking of the broom across the studio floor as David swept.

She could hear everything that went on in the studio above her head, and liked to sit and listen to Ari's lessons through the muffle of the insulation and old wood. She could pick out songs, and said their titles aloud as she moved through the house. "Paganini," she'd say to herself as she rinsed the breakfast dishes. "Concerto in D Major." And then later in the lesson, the chapel piece for the week, usually Bach.

Ari was good. Even Bente could tell. He was David's first prodigy.

"The boy's a genius with the violin," David had told her the first day he heard Ari play. "He could become something great."

David was as new to the seminary as Ari, and as diligent. In the mornings he dressed and ate quickly, disappeared up to the studio before Bente awoke, leaving her the last of the coffee still in the pot, and his breakfast dishes piled in the sink. When she awoke, he was always already playing, the stringed sound of his violin entering the bedroom through the ceiling, trembling inside the walls.

The house was part of David's professorship. It sat below the limestone buildings of the campus, in a row with other faculty houses, across from the orchard. It was old, the porch drooping with age and dry rot, but it was the violinist's house, David explained when they first visited the campus. They could not refuse it.

On the front lawn a sign read Buxtehude House, for the composer, because the seminary was Lutheran.

"Buxtehude," Bente said on that first visit. "I read Bach traveled two hundred miles on foot to hear him play." This was the kind of thing she knew, a needless tidbit of a fact she had read and tucked into her mind to save. She turned, but David had wandered around the side of the house and was on the landing at the top of the staircase, jangling the lock on the studio door. "The organ," she said to herself, and followed him. "Bach wanted to hear him play the organ."

When they moved into the house later in the summer, Bente found little remains of the last professor's life tucked into the bureau drawers and beneath the bed. In the bookshelf, along with textbooks and sheet music and four copies of *Luther's Small Catechism*, Bente discovered a row of paperbacks, a book of illustrations titled *The Sixteen Pleasures*, a leather-bound volume of *Lolita*. In the drawer of the bedside table, someone had forgotten his reading glasses, a tube of ointment. And a knot of long, white hair tangled the mouth of the tub drain in the bathroom. Bente carried the books out to the back porch and left them there. She threw the eyeglasses into the trash, and took a butter knife to the drain, the white mineral cake on the metal chipping off on the tip of the blade as she freed the knot.

Sometimes Bente imagined what it would be like for her to leave David alone with the house and just go. She listed in her mind the things she would need to pack: her clothes and a book or two, the pillowcases her grandmother had embroidered for her wedding. She would take her comb and the tube of toothpaste and leave David to buy his own. Bente stood at the kitchen sink and watched the reflection of her face in the dark window as she thought about these things.

Occasionally in the fantasy she left without taking any of it, just going, suddenly, running down the road with her coat hem flapping at her sides. Other times she took it all. Even the violin.

Once Ari began lessons, David's hours in the studio lasted until midnight or dawn, and Bente stopped waiting up for him. She crawled into bed and pulled the blankets close to her chin. Iowa was colder than she had imagined it would be, a brittle kind of cold that frosted the windows of the house and the branches of the orchard across the street, and the nights seemed longer and blacker, the quiet wider.

Bente lay listening to the music above her head during one of Ari's early lessons. "Ravel's Rhapsody," she whispered as she folded herself into the mass of blankets and turned off the bedside lamp. The sound of the two violins together rose and fell above the ceiling, then David stopped, and she heard only Ari's violin still playing, the notes clear and vibrating against the glass of the bedroom window. She fell asleep to the playing and only half woke up when David finally came down to bed. She could smell the scent of pine rosin on his hand then, the stinging copper scent of violin strings on his fingers.

The first snow of the winter fell later in the week, and Bente was glad she'd already picked the apples. When she woke up in the morning, the house was quiet; she listened for David playing upstairs, and when she didn't hear him, she got up and went to the kitchen. From the window she could see that it had snowed all night, piling the window ledge with several inches and burying the yard. The snow had stopped falling, but when the breeze gusted, skiffs rose up from the lawn and sifted and glittered in the gray morning light. David had cleared the stairs to the studio and the railings, and Bente saw the holes his boots had left in the snow, trailing around the house to the front. She tied her robe closed and walked out to the front porch.

"What are you doing?" she called to him where he stood with a trench shovel and a broom at the end of the drive.

He'd put on his coat, but beneath it, the drape of his bathrobe dragged through the snow, and his pajama pants were tucked into the tops of his boots. "We need to buy a snow shovel," he said. He smiled at her, and she could see his breath as he plunged the narrow scoop of the trench shovel back down into the snow and brought up a small heap. "This is going to take all day," he laughed.

For a moment she remembered him, the way he'd been when she'd first met him. How certain she once had been about being his wife. She moved to sit down on the first step of the stoop, her bare feet tucked up beneath her body to keep warm.

David dropped the shovel into the snow and came to sit down beside her. "I should cancel the day," he said. "Just call a snow day. Build a snowman, like a kid." He folded the bathrobe over his legs and pressed his gloved hands between his knees.

"I like this," Bente said, "this much snow. I've never seen so much." She looked across the street to where the apple trees were heavy with snow. The last of the apples hung like bright ornaments from the branches. "We should walk through the orchard later, once I get dressed." She leaned near him, so that her shoulder touched his.

"Bente, you know I can't really cancel." He kissed her cheek and stood up. "Take a walk, though, so you can tell me about it. I'll be waiting all day to hear."

Ari was the only student to show up for lessons that day. He arrived on skis, white faced from the cold and bundled into snow pants and a parka, its furred hood pulled up and cinched beneath his chin. She saw him fumble to free his boots from the buckles, then poke the skis into an upright X in the snow near the stairway. *Hello,* he mouthed to her through the kitchen window as he passed it. She didn't smile, just watched him lumber his way up the steps to the studio.

Once they began playing, Bente put on her own coat and boots and wandered across the street into the orchard. She thought about going back and taking Ari's skis, cutting a neat, bladed path through the snow. But she kept walking instead, beneath the bare branches of the trees near the road, toward the far side of the orchard, where there were just the blackened stumps of trees that had been burned. When she reached the stumps, Bente brushed the snow from one and sat down, broke a piece of the charred bark into her hand. She'd seen an orchard burn as a child, on a hill above her grandmother's house in eastern Washington. The trees were dry wood and burned fast. The smoke they put off roiled above the orchard thick and blue, and there was the smell of apple blossoms still in the ash that the wind carried into town days later.

She'd told David the story once, when they were still new to one another and to each other's stories.

"How horrible," he said. "All those trees just going to waste."

Bente looked away. "I remember it, though—that's not waste."

David reached across the table to take her hand in his. His hands were warm, his fingers careful, but rough at their tips. (Later, once they were married, Bente would sometimes tense suddenly beneath him in bed at the cut of his touch, the surprising slice of a callus as his fingers moved over her.) "It's not as if remembering brings things to life again, Bente. Of course you remember," he smiled, pressed her hand. "But the trees were already just dust."

In the orchard, Bente stood up and toed the stump so that a black peppering of char splintered off and dusted the snow at its base. She walked back toward the house, and when she reached the road, saw David in his coat and boots, standing on the other side.

"I was just about to come find you," he said. He kept his hands in the pockets of his coat. "I guess I've missed the walk."

Bente stepped across the ditch and met him in front of the house. "Lesson's over?"

David nodded. "I told him we'd work harder tomorrow, no evening lessons tonight." He smiled, waiting for her to smile too, she could see, to put her arms around his neck, thank him. "Walk with me," he said, and motioned to the orchard.

Bente unwrapped the scarf from her neck, undid the button at the throat of her coat. "I'm cold, David," she said. She turned away from him and started for the house. "I'm going in to take a bath now."

David stood at the edge of the yard, unmoving, as if she might change her mind.

But from the porch Bente looked at him and said, "You go ahead and keep working." She unlaced her boots and took them in her hand. The treads were full of melting snow and dripped on the slats of the porch floor. "Call Ari," she said, opening the front door. "I'm sure he'll come back."

Inside, in the bathroom, Bente undressed and ran a bath. When the tub had filled, she turned off the faucet and slid into the water. She could hear David above her, playing again already, something she recognized but could not name. Almost a dirge, she thought, the music gray and unlively.

Saturday afternoon it began to snow again. Bente watched the sky through the window as she worked on dinner. She'd frozen the apples she'd picked, saving them for Ari's pie, and had searched her cookbook for a recipe. When David returned from the store, she was rolling out a crust.

"It's coming down out there," David said. He set his grocery bag on the counter and dusted the shoulders of his jacket, his hair.

"I see that."

"You're making pie," he said, incredulous, and grinned. "Have you made a pie before?"

"I have a recipe," Bente said. She dropped the rolling pin to the counter, flattened the round of dough. "Anyone can make a pie. It's nothing special."

"She cooks!" he joked. "She bakes!" David pulled a wine bottle and a bag of salad greens from the sack and set them on the counter. "I'm teasing," he said. "You know I'm teasing." He touched her shoulder as he left the room.

Once the pie was in the oven, Bente moved through the house straightening. She shifted the pillows on the couch, held them out in front of her with rigid arms and beat them fat again, then smoothed the afghan some other professor's wife had knitted and left on the back of the living room couch. She wiped the table down, and slid in her stocking feet across the dark wood of the narrow entryway once or twice, to polish it. These were not her things and she didn't care; Ari was not her student. She could hear David above her head, playing for the fourth time since lunch a Vivaldi piece she'd tired of even before he'd begun it. Her mother had owned a record of *The Four Seasons* and several Vivaldi concerti that she'd played over and over on their stereo set when Bente was young, and it seemed this afternoon that Bente had heard enough of Vivaldi to play him herself. "David!" She opened the front door and yelled up to him finally, but he didn't hear her, and she turned to go back inside, feeling silly, rageful. "Violin Concerto number six," she said as she closed the door and went to get dressed.

Ari knocked on the door at six-thirty, his skis locked together in his hand and his face again tucked into the mass of his hood. "I'm early," he said when Bente opened the door.

"No," she said, polite. "Of course not. I have the table all ready."

He laid his skis on the porch and carried his violin under his arm, setting it on the floor between his feet to take off his coat, as if he were in danger of her grabbing it from him, snatching it away. She'd seen David stand so protectively over his case too. It reminded her of a dog with a bone, and she wanted to laugh a moment, looking at skinny Ari with his chaos of scarf and mittens, guarding the violin. She wondered if he had always had the quirk, or if it was something David had passed on to him already, his progeny, his son.

"Too much snow," she said. "It's a hassle just to cross the street."

Ari looked at her and laughed. He had a wispy kind of laugh, more air than anything else. "But the farmers need it, right?"

Bente took his coat and sent him through the back door to find David. It was dark out already, and dark in the house, and she walked through the hallway and front room turning on lamps, striking a match to light the candles she had set out on the dining room table.

"This is nice," Ari said to Bente when he and David appeared at the back door again. "The work you've done."

David smiled, crossed the room to pull her chair out for her. "She isn't very experienced at this, are you, sweetheart? Neither of us is particularly domestic." He bent and kissed the top of her head. "We've become experts at ramen noodles and macaroni."

Ari took his seat and unfolded the blue napkin Bente had placed beside his plate. He kept his eyes on her, and then, briefly, looked down.

Saying his own grace, Bente thought, and said sharply, "Let's get started then. I'm sure Ari's starved."

They passed the bowls of potatoes and green beans, and David stood with the carving knife, slicing the roast before forking a piece of meat onto each plate and sitting down to his own. He and Ari began a conversation about the winter concert piece they were working on, a difficult Stravinsky concerto that David said he'd picked especially for Ari. "None of the others could handle it," he said, and turned to the boy.

"Thank you," Ari said. He looked down at his hands, but grinned. "I'm only playing to play, though. And I'm still not sure I want to do that piece at the concert. I'd like to just be part of the orchestra."

David laughed. "Part of the orchestra!"

Bente wondered if this was just how it went with them, this flattery and mock humility, an ugly sort of tennis match they liked to play with one another.

"Honestly," Ari said, and flushed finally, severely. "I'm not sure I want to do the piece."

Bente looked across the table at David. The muscle at his temple tightened and he nodded. He'd been in such good spirits all evening, cutting the roast and carrying on as he had about his own playing, the musicians he'd worked with. She wanted suddenly to reach across the table and lay her hand on his, comfort him.

They'd hosted a dinner once for a group of friends before they were married, and David had been clumsy and quiet. He'd spilled his wine on her tablecloth and then begun a joke without remembering its punchline. There'd been a silence around the table then until Bente laughed. She took his left hand in hers beneath the table, rubbed her thumb against the calluses of his fingers. She knew she would not abandon him. She would look after him because, in that moment, she was certain she was the kind of woman who could.

Bente stood up. "I'm getting the pie," she said, and began reaching across the table, stacking the dishes to carry into the kitchen.

"Let me help you with that." Ari pushed back in his seat to get up.

"I've got it," Bente said, terse and louder than she meant to be, stopping him. She braced a plate between her arm and her body and moved toward the kitchen, leaving them to go on talking.

It was quiet in the kitchen, and through the black glass of the window, she could see the shadows of snowflakes still falling. She had never seen so much snow. They could be snowed in entirely, she thought. They could be stuck in the house until March, the doors and the windows unable to open, and the ground beneath the snow outside softening to mud.

"Are you sure you don't want help?" Ari asked. He had gotten up from the table and stood in the doorway, his hands in his pockets.

Bente turned. "I'm just going to get the pie out and start some coffee. You and David can talk."

"He went out." Ari nodded toward the front door. "To check the snow. It's getting pretty thick out there," he said. "It might be too much for my skis. I'll have to walk."

You should have thought of that before, Bente wanted to say. He wasn't going to stay the night, if that's what he was asking of her. "You'll have quite an adventure getting home," she said, and turned to open the refrigerator for the pie, leaning forward into the cool air inside.

"I guess the skis will probably be fine then," he said. "But David thought I could leave my violin."

Bente stood up with the pie in her arms, reached to the drawer for the knife. "Your violin?"

"The cold. He said it isn't a good idea to let the wood get too cold."

"Right," Bente said. "Whatever you want to do." She brushed past him into the dining room and set the pie in the center of the table.

He stood in the doorway, watching her. "I do appreciate it," he said. "His attention."

Bente set down the knife and silver pie server. She turned to face him and saw that he was blushing again, that he'd embarrassed himself being so forward. "I saw David play once," she said. "It was before we were married, and he was playing at a church." He'd been in an orchestra, as young then as Ari was now. He'd worn a black tuxedo, and the rosin shook out around his shoulders like a spray of sparks, then landed in a white dust on the fabric of his jacket sleeves. "It was night," Bente went on, "and there were candles in the church, right in front of where David was playing."

She could see past the boy and into the kitchen. The warm water she'd filled the sink with had heated the window above it, and beads of condensation had formed on the glass.

The flush in Ari's face had faded, and he leaned against the doorjamb, smirking, fierce and adolescent. Ari said, "And you thought David was a genius."

Bente looked away. "No," she said. "I was going to say he was just like you."

The house was silent, packed in the snow, but she could hear David stomping off his boots on the porch, opening the front door. "One thing so easily becomes another sometimes, doesn't it?" she said. She turned back around to the table then, leaned over to cut the pie.

It was nearly midnight when Ari left, and Bente and David stood on the porch as he strapped on his skis in the front yard and waved good-bye to them. The snow had stopped momentarily, and the sky was the muddy purple of winter nights, of a storm about to arrive or of one just quieting.

"Dinner was nice," David said, leaning to press his shoulder against hers. "The pie was different. It wasn't sweet."

"The apples were the ones from the orchard."

"I wouldn't use them again," David said. He put his arm around her waist. Through her coat she could not feel the warmth of his arm against her, just its press.

"No," Bente said. "They weren't what I had hoped."

They stood beside one another on the porch, the heat of their breath rising in clouds, cooling, disappearing in the night air above their heads. They watched Ari's figure glide away smoothly on top of the snow on the road, both of them still listening for the clear and certain whisking sound of his skis long after he was gone from their sight.

Lucidity

Ben says they will stop and buy a cake on the way home—a big cake, two layers, with seven candles for seven years of marriage, and pink champagne if she likes—but first they must do this, they must move Gisela out of her home. "I promise," he says, and leans toward Annie, his eyes still on the road, his hand on her bare knee, fingers working the hem of her green skirt slowly up her thigh.

Annie lays her own hand down on his. "Ben," she says to stop him, and straightens her skirt. The car tires stutter over the ribs of cement beneath them, and Annie feels the rattle under her skin, a tremor like a tiny earthquake rippling through her nerves. She shivers and Ben reaches forward to adjust the heat in the car.

It is winter still, and not warm, but the San Francisco sun is out, the sky the faint blue of old china, or of a faded linen tablecloth Annie remembers from childhood. The sky is unwrinkled and cloudless, and when the car crests the curve of the bridge, she sees that the bay is just as smooth, but dark and glinting like polished obsidian.

"Your mother," Annie says. "Is she expecting us? Did you call to say we were coming?" She turns her head to the window, watches squares of city pass between the metal slats of the bridge beams.

The pack of buildings looks small and crowded onto its strip of land across the water.

"I'll take her out with me," Ben says. "I'll take her to the bakery she likes, get her out of the house while you pack her bags."

It feels like a crime the way Ben has organized his mother's move, and he has made Annie the criminal. At the door, after the hugs and fumbled greetings, he will tell Gisela they've come to take her out on the town. An afternoon away, he'll say. We're taking you to lunch, Mamma.

And then Annie will beg off—a headache, suddenly. One of her migraines. She will drop herself into one of Gisela's wide, ivory armchairs and touch her temples with careful fingertips, her eyes squeezed shut. Please, go without me, she'll say. I just need to lie down in the dark awhile.

Gisela will not remember that it is Annie and Ben's anniversary. She may not even remember Annie's name. The last time they visited, the old woman shuffled around the house for an hour before remembering where she had left the plate of cookies she'd made for the visit, then found them, finally, in the bathroom towel closet, along with a dozen spoiled eggs still in their carton and the book she'd been reading. Sometimes lately, Gisela could not remember to turn off her coffeepot in the morning. Often, she could not remember how to climb once she reached the steep angle of steps leading from the street up to her lawn. The neighbors had begun to phone. "She's doing it again," one said to Annie, impatient as with a misbehaving dog. "She's standing in the street again, just looking at the steps. You have to come and get her. You have to do something.

One of us is going to hit her in the road, and whose fault will it be?"
Annie did not say thank you, but simply set the phone back down
into its cradle, hung up.

"Is this fair?" Annie turns to him in the driver's seat and asks.
She doesn't say what she means: Is this fair *today?* Is it fair to me to
do this today?

Ben sits straight-backed and says nothing, turns the car off
the bridge and onto a street of little shops, a delicatessen with its
yellow awning aged by wind and salt-and-city air. The plum trees
along the sidewalk are just blooming and their blossoms seem to
float, bunched but unattached. When she first moved to California,
to be with Ben, Annie noticed the oddity of the plum trees, their
strange contradiction—the white, bridal froth of the blossoms, and
the bodily, masculine scent they put off.

This morning Ben woke her by bending over her in their
bed, blowing against her neck, her earlobe, until she startled from
whatever dream it was she'd been having and opened her eyes. He
smiled, kissed her forehead, and sat back, his legs straddling her
own. Annie closed her eyes again but did not tell him to move, to
let her up to go to the bathroom. If it had been any other day she
would have rolled over, groaned at him to leave her to her sleep, but
she saw in his face how he was trying.

"It's our day," he said. He picked up her arm, kissed the inside
of her elbow. Seven years and he still believed this was how she
liked to be awakened.

In the car, she reaches for his hand again. He looks young—
even younger today it seems. Behind his round glasses, his eyes are

bright as blue glass, and there is only the small streak of white in his blond hair, a tuft, like Gisela's, at his forehead. Gisela's hair is still as fair as his, just the one shoot of white, which she weaves into the long braid she twines every morning around her head. It is the way she has worn her hair since Annie met her—since ever, Ben has said.

"We don't have to do this today," Annie says. "Another bed will open up for her later, if we wait."

Ben slips his fingers from hers. "We're in the city now, Annie," he says. "I have to pay attention."

He has dragged his feet about Gisela's disease, left to Annie the preparations that have led to this day. At the Oak Hill Adult Care Center, where they will leave Gisela tonight, he walked uneasily behind the attendant the day they first toured the building, the brochure Annie had given him earlier folded and tucked into the back pocket of his pants. "This place doesn't smell like I thought it would," he said to the young attendant, and she smiled, looked to Annie as if she hadn't understood him, but nodded. Her name tag read *Maria-Terese*, and Annie wondered if she'd been picked to guide these tours because of the saintliness of the name, as if to assure people their loved ones would have blessed ends. She wore a starched and thick white apron, orderly as the white buckets lining the hallways, hiding the diapers, the stained bedsheets and towels, the smell Ben had been expecting.

There were railings along the walls, and Annie stepped around patients pushing themselves an inch at a time in wheelchairs or walkers toward their bedrooms. At the end of one hallway, a woman in a blue nightgown stood at her walker, weeping.

"I want to leave," Ben stepped close to Annie and whispered. He folded his arms across his chest, holding himself.

"We have to take care of her, Ben," Annie said. "This is the best way to take care of her." She reached out and put her hand in his. "This is age."

Oak Hill was close, not in the city, where they would have to drive two hours just to visit Gisela on a Sunday afternoon; they could drop in every day if they wanted to, Ben said later, convincing himself. His brother Peder could drive up from Los Angeles in a day, it was not too far. He told Annie this the night after their tour. He sat at the table with a pad of paper and his calculator, wrote in his messy hand the cost of the care center, the numbers of his mother's pension, the figure she still received each month from his father's retirement, the amount he guessed they could make off her house.

Annie stood at the sink as he wrote. She dipped her hands into the water and brought up a wineglass, a plate from dinner. She worked on the silver tines of a salad fork with the bristles of her scrub brush. The bubbles of dish soap had gone flat, the water gray, and beneath the surface her hands were also gray, the color of pale clay, the skin thin and her veins raised by the heat. She found herself looking at the skin of her hands—of her face and neck—all the time lately, looking for she didn't know what. Age spots maybe? The antiqued, papery look of Gisela's skin? She had been too young to pay attention to her own mother's aging, and by the time she would have liked to ask what it was to be a wife, a mother, to be no longer young exactly, her mother was already gone.

Her mother was the fragile sort of woman, though. She wore sun hats in June and pearls all winter. She did not work, often not even at home, and as a child Annie could nearly always find her tucked up under the afghan on the sofa for a nap, or on her bed, her eyes closed beneath a damp cloth. "Are you sick?" Annie asked, that familiar stone of fear sinking in her center. And then her mother's cool touch on Annie's wrist, a little push with the tips of her fingers to say *Go*. "Resting my eyes," her mother would say, and turn slightly. "Go find something to do, Anne."

Once, in the summer, her mother took her swimming in the lake near her grandparents' house in Minnesota, and when the towel fell from her mother's waist to her feet, Annie saw that the dough-white skin at the backs of her knees was netted in a fine purple lace of veins, proof that she really was more fragile than everyone else. As if when she slid into the water, the last transparent film of skin would slide from her, allow her to finally dissolve as she'd always threatened to do.

Gisela would never be described as fragile. Her body was solid beneath the starched white men's shirts and long canvas skirts she liked to wear, her voice was deep, as if she pulled it up from her toes each time she spoke. She never wore gloves when she gardened, and her hands had taken on the stain of the soil, the skin of her palms like a pale brown crust of bread, her nails thickened from use.

The night Ben first brought Annie to the house in the city to meet his mother, Gisela greeted them at the door. She reached for Ben's face and held it in her two hands, kissed his cheeks and then his forehead. *"Hur mår du? Hur mår du?"* she whispered as she kissed him.

"Fine. Fine," Ben said. He leaned into her like a little boy, Annie thought, and looked politely away.

Gisela had made dinner for them, white potatoes with dill and butter, cod, and a blackberry pie. Gisela settled herself in the chair beside Ben's, touched his arm as she ate, leaning toward him. She seemed to take up the whole room by just being in it, not to swallow up the space, but to crowd it. They ate without speaking, without music on the stereo in the other room.

"Get the coffee, Bengt," Gisela finally said when they finished the meal.

When he left, Gisela turned her face to Annie. "I see he loves you," she said. "He's loved others." She pushed her seat back and stood up to serve the pie, unbuttoning the first button of her shirt before leaning over the table, tucking in the long ends of her green scarf. "Blackberry stains do not come out," she explained. She slid a piece of pie onto a dessert plate, licked her thumb as she offered the slice to Annie.

Annie wanted to get up then and follow Ben into the kitchen, have a moment with him to herself. Your mother, she wanted to say. She has such bite. But she sat still in her seat, her foot ticking out a nervous rhythm beneath the table as she smiled, and took the pie.

Later, in Ben's bedroom, in his apartment across the bay, Annie lay back on his bed. "Does she always kiss you that way?" Annie asked. "When you visit, does she always hold your arm during dinner?" She pressed her fingers to Ben's arm herself, put her face to his shoulder. She could smell the scrubbed scent of Gisela still on him. She had been seeing Gisela in his face all night.

"She's lonely," Ben said. He reached to turn off the lamp, then reached for Annie. The city sounded beyond the apartment window, a siren and someone on the corner shouting to herself, the highway noise that could nearly be mistaken for wind.

"She doesn't like me," Annie said. "She won't learn to like me."

"Quiet," Ben said gently. "She's not here now." He leaned over Annie, bent down toward her. She winced when she felt his teeth at her breast.

Now, at the corner, Ben turns the car onto Gisela's street and parks. "Okay," he says. "You know what to do." He touches Annie's hand, smiles. "Tonight we'll have our anniversary," he says. "I promise." He gets out, and Annie watches him disappear up the steps to Gisela's yard. She expects him to turn, to stop when he notices she isn't behind him and to wait for her to get out of the car and follow, but he doesn't notice, and in a moment she's certain he's inside the house already, receiving Gisela's kisses and not coming for her. She steps out of the car and stands on the sidewalk a moment, smoothing her skirt, then begins up the steps.

From the top of the steps, Gisela's garden spreads out, the flowers just opening, their specks of winter color pale, and above them, near the house, the white umbrella of the plum in blossom. Gisela had wanted them to marry underneath that tree, and when Annie said no, they'd be married in the church, Gisela stiffened.

She turned to Ben. "Already leashing you, I see," she said. And then, "That's fine." She looked to Annie. "I'm sure it will all be just what you've hoped."

Along the garden, Gisela has dug a small trench and planted it with bulbs. Tulips, pale yellow and peach, milky white and pink, and beside them, the last of the crocuses. Nearly every weekend she calls Ben to come and help her with the garden, to mow the lawn or tug weeds or help with the tilling. Annie hears him on the phone Saturday mornings, early, before the sun is even full in the window of their bedroom.

"Where is Peder?" Annie asked when he came in the last time to wake her, to get ready to drive into the city. "You're not her only son."

"You know he can't drive up from LA to help her weed." Ben turned his back to her and pulled a tee shirt over his head. "Besides, he's busy."

"So are you," Annie said. "You have a wife, you remember." She looked away from him. "You'll let her ruin us," she said. She wanted to hurt him.

Ben walked to her and leaned over the bed. "I won't talk to you about this now," he said. He kissed her forehead in the way she had seen him kiss Gisela's—formal, careful of her and her anger. She wondered if he felt he was tolerating her in the same way he tolerated his mother, if she reminded him just then of Gisela, some-how, and if she had reminded him of Gisela before, before they were married and when he met her. She rolled her body away from him and waited for him to leave her.

At Gisela's house, Annie opens the front door and steps inside. She can hear Ben's voice and Gisela's in the kitchen, but she stands in the hallway, her purse on her elbow, wet grass clinging to the sides of her white pumps. The house smells polished, like lemon oil and the lye Gisela still uses to clean. At the window, the sheer drapery has been pulled back, and the late morning light is coming in white and washed, glinting off the hardwood of the floors. The new owners will want to take those curtains down, Annie thinks. They will want to strip the wood where it has been over-scrubbed and is paler, to re-stain it a warmer color, re-paint the white walls a creamy shade of apricot or buttery yellow. They will want to rip out Gisela's garden in the back, replace it with sea grass or ice plant like the rest of the neighbors have done, let it slowly take over the yard so that there will be less work to do.

Annie drops her purse to the floor and leans back against the front door. She wants to go back out to the car, wait for Ben to find her. *It's our anniversary*, she'll say when he does. She shouldn't have to say anything more.

Suddenly, Gisela's blond head appears at the doorway to the kitchen. "I wondered if you had come too," she says. She sounds lucid. Her words are in order. She recognizes Annie.

Ben is behind her, looking at Annie. She can see on his face that Gisela is having a good day. His eyes are wide, like a boy caught. *It will be harder this way*, Annie knows he is thinking. *Yes, and you deserve it*, she wants to say back to him. But he looks so frightened too, not just guilty, but afraid. His hand is on his mother's shoulder, as if to steady her. Annie touched her own mother that way, often, the days when her mother was well, when she seemed somehow more solidly alive. Annie touched her then just as Ben is touching Gisela now, not just to hold onto her mother, but to hold her own fear an arm's length away.

Annie picks up her purse and steps away from the door and into the room. She smiles at Gisela. "Of course I came too," she says. "I'm sorry I didn't come in right away, but I think I feel a headache coming on." She looks to Ben, releases him. She will take care of it. She'll let him leave her to take care of it.

Gisela sees their car pull up from the front window. She was not expecting them. She turns and steps away. "So, it comes to this," she says to herself. She runs her palms down the front of her shirt, straightens her skirt, and raises a hand to tuck a strand of fallen hair back into the crown of her braid. She was able to braid her hair this morning. She was able to undress and climb into the porcelain tub. To wash herself. To fill and lift the white jug of water she uses to rinse the shampoo from her hair without forgetting why she has filled it, without struggling over just how to get the water to come pouring out.

She had sat naked at the dressing table in the bedroom afterward, wet still, but not because she had forgotten to dry, because it was lovely out this morning. The sun in the room was white and brilliant and glimmering, as if it too had been poured and was dripping from her skin. She sat for a long time and admired the way the light flashed off her wet shoulders. Then, finally, she reached up as she has always done, and braided her hair quickly, agile fingered, wound it around her head and placed the pins. The silence in the house was as white as the light, and when she went to the window, still without her clothes, and pushed it up to feel the air, she saw that more had bloomed in the garden since yesterday (she remembered what had been open and what had not). She saw that the bay beyond the rooftops of her neighbors' houses and the city was a pool of black ink spilled and sparkling, and she thought of inkwells then. She thought of the fountain pen Nils had used to write her love letters when they were young, and of the heel of his hand stained with a tattoo of ink that looked like the dark petals of a flower spreading on the skin. Sometimes it seems she is not forgetting but remembering too much, so much that she cannot move through the day as she is expected to, but has to sit and stare and let her mind take its time. *Lucidity*, her son calls it when she looks most awake to him. But she thinks, No, it is not lucidity, it is boredom. On those lucid days it is as if each moment were flat enough to slide against the next and slip away, none more important than the other, none interesting to her anymore, or, at least, not as interesting as the more languid, dreaming moments of her non-lucid days. She feels like she is swimming then, when she is lost in her mind, and it is as pleasant as peaceful sleep.

"Bengt," she says when her son opens the front door. She reaches to hug him and smells the honeyed scent of his wife's perfume. "Where is your wife?" she asks. She closes the door behind him. He has moved into the front room and is plucking lemon drops from the white glass bowl she keeps on the mantel. Still a boy, she thinks without pleasure. He is past thirty, her youngest son, and still fishing candies from the dish. He will expect her to make lunch. He will want to sit beside her and watch her eat. Gisela knows that her neighbors call him, that they report to him as if he were her guardian, and that this has made him watchful of her, the way he was when he was small, always keeping an eye on everyone, not to be left out ever, or left behind. She moves through the front room to the kitchen and yells out, "Are you thirsty? I can make tea. I'll make you tea."

In the kitchen she fills the kettle and sets it on the stove to boil, then finds the tea and spoons it into the mesh basket of the strainer. She pours the last of the milk from the refrigerator into the pewter server and sets it on the table beside its sister sugar bowl— her mother's set, from Sweden. She would pass these on if she had a daughter, but she has only men behind her, and Anne—she refuses to say Annie, as her son does, as if his wife were a ridiculous comic strip character. "Where is your wife?" she asks again as he pulls a chair out at the kitchen table and sits down.

"I thought we'd take you out today, Mamma," he says. His grin is his father's, wide, boyish. "Coffee, or lunch if you like."

"That's fine," she says. She picks up the kettle just before it begins to scream and fills his teacup. "Don't burn," she says, and hands it to him, blowing ripples across the red surface of the tea.

She sits across from him with her own cup. *Milk*, she thinks, and pours, sets the milk back on the table. *Sugar. Stir.* She forces the words to form in her mind, then follows their directions. Bengt watches her from his place, his teacup steaming between his two big hands. If she forgets anything—the second spoon of sugar, the stirring—if she spills or prepares her tea and then does not drink it, he will notice. He will hold these little snags of memory against her. "You see," she says as she sets her cup down. "Tea in the morning is always good." She waits for him to relax, to ease back against his chair, and he does.

When he was a boy, he was her little ally. Peder was the struggle, Bengt the reward. She took them to the water often, after school, when they were finally freed from the classroom and nearly quaking to get outside and run around in the sun. Peder would swing out of the car as soon as it was stopped, and run down the beach, arms and legs wild to leave her. Bengt tried to follow him but was slower. She had time to say, "Look! Look at your brother, flapping like a silly bird out there!" She laughed, touched Bengt's knee to let him in on her joke. "We'll just go sit in the sun like civilized people, won't we." And he would stay with her, building dry heaps of sand castles to smash all around the edge of her beach blanket.

Peder has Los Angeles now, and Bengt has Anne.

"I should check on her," Bengt says, and pushes back his chair. "Annie. She's still in the car I think." He stands up, pink-faced.

"Old for a tantrum, I'd say." Gisela presses her lips together, stops herself from saying any more, and stands up too, walks out to the front room ahead of him. Anne is at the front door, stopped and still, and it is a moment before she raises her eyes to meet Gisela's. "I wondered if you had come too," Gisela says.

"Of course I came too." Anne smiles, touches her forehead. The pistachio-colored purse she's carrying swings at her elbow and slides down toward her shoulder. It matches her skirt and the cardigan she's wearing. She's a tidy woman. Gisela has always thought that of her—at least she is tidy. She wears her dark hair pulled back severely, and it makes her small face seem sharper than it probably is, sharp in a way that makes Gisela think of birds, thin-boned and moving in that jerky, mechanical way that is not unlike how her daughter-in-law moves, nervously, out of sync with her body in the way only a childless woman can be. "I'm sorry I didn't come in right away," Anne says, still touching at her forehead, "but I think I feel a headache coming on."

"Well," Bengt's voice is flat. His hand is warm on Gisela's shoulder, firm. She sees this is the part he has rehearsed. "We were going to go out."

Gisela would like to remind him that she is *lucid* today, that she is his mother, regardless. But instead she nods. She turns to her son and smiles, sharply. "Bengt, you go and get us lunch and bring it back here. Your wife is ill and she can't go out."

The color flares again in his face, and he looks to Anne. She bends to set her purse down on the floor and says in a voice of resignation, "Yes, Ben. Go get lunch."

All three stand without moving. The light coming in through the window shifts, and the room dims and brightens, dims. The leafed shadow of the Japanese quince beyond the window trembles on the wall with an unfelt breeze.

"All right," Bengt says, and steps around Gisela. He goes without kissing her or Anne, and the two women sit still and quiet until the sound of his car can't be heard, and then Gisela stands up.

"So the day isn't quite what you planned," she begins. She sighs, and moves back into the kitchen, where she collects the teacups and saucers from the table. She goes to stand at the sink and turns on the faucet to wash them. If she were to leave, she would not take any of her things. She would leave her mother's pewter coffee set, the china she was given for her trousseau, all of Nils's letters that she keeps in the hatbox beneath the bed upstairs. (She will forget that these things have been left anyhow. Eventually, she knows, she will forget.)

"Do you need help?" Anne says from the doorway. She has come in and is watching Gisela. "You're not holding the cup under the water. You haven't got any soap."

Her voice is thin as her bony shoulders, Gisela thinks, and turns to face her daughter-in-law. "I was daydreaming," she says. "Don't forget to mention it to my son. He's keeping track."

Anne goes to the table and sits down.

When Bengt first brought Anne home, Gisela watched how she moved and sat and ate. She was stiff, careful as if waiting for shards of the sky to come slicing down around her. Bengt waits, Gisela thought, but that one, she waits for disaster. At dessert, Gisela stood up to refill the coffee cups and disturbed the tablecloth as she moved so that her fork jumped from the table. Anne caught it in one quick reach and replaced it beside Gisela's napkin. Of course, Gisela thought. Of course she caught it.

At the table now, Anne swipes crumbs from the tabletop into her open palm and holds them there.

"I haven't cleaned," Gisela says. "You weren't expected today."

"We should have called," Anne says. "I thought Ben had."

"My husband left those things to me too."

"It was just a whim," Anne says. She fists her palm around the crumbs and does not raise her eyes to Gisela's. "We thought it was nice out, nice day for a trip to the city."

"Whatever seemed unpleasant. He left those things to me."

"The weather is very pleasant today," Anne says. She lifts her chin now, smiles. "The day is pleasant. It's our anniversary."

Anne rises and the hem of her skirt falls around her knees. Gisela thinks of the drapery in the front room, the way the light dropped to a small, flickering line on the floor when she let the drapery slide from her fingers as she stood at the window watching Bengt come up the walk. When she and Nils bought the house, he had argued with her about that window, wanting to take it out. It would let too much light in, he argued. It would let the neighbors see the goings-on of the household. It was too wide, too exposing. They should replace it with a wall and buy lamps. But the garden beyond it was already growing in Gisela's mind, and she could see the purple buds of wisteria butting against the window, the dappled heads of daylilies with their tongues out, about to lick the glass. There was always the fight and then the giving in.

She had the wall he built knocked back out just after he died, the window replaced. (Funny to give in as she had, so easily, just to release him from the argument. To prefer her own displeasure over his.)

"Gisela," Anne says. She is standing close. Her hand is at Gisela's elbow. "You've drifted," she says.

Gisela turns her face to Anne, hands her the last teacup to dry and put away, and walks to the table to sit down. "He's left you with me on your anniversary," she says.

"We'll celebrate later. He'll buy a cake."

"Yes," Gisela says. "He'll buy a cake so that you'll forgive him this. Or so that he can forgive himself this, that's more likely the reason." She leans back in her chair. She is tired. She would like to climb the stairs and lie down on her bed, feel the nubbed pattern of the white chenille spread under her palms. She'd like it if Anne had gone off too and left her. "You should have gone with him," she says. "He might be gone awhile, and now you're here."

"You understand this," Anne says, her voice even, suddenly stern. She crosses the kitchen and sits in the chair beside Gisela's. "You can't be alone. You can't stay here alone."

"On my seventh wedding anniversary—you see I haven't forgotten it all—Bengt was new. We'd just that week come home from the hospital. I expected him to be the kind of baby Peder had been—colicky, crying all the time. He wasn't, though. He was silent. At my breast he was silent, filling himself with me. At night, he slept beside me on the bed, and sometimes, when I woke up, I would find him watching me, his eyes open, though he'd never made a sound."

"He watches me when I sleep now," Anne says.

"You can't understand what I mean."

Anne looks away, presses her folded hands against the table-top. "There are memories in this house. You want to hold on to them," she says. "I can understand that."

Gisela stands up. "You're afraid the house lets him hold on to me." She smiles, grips the back of her chair. Her knees feel soft as lumps of butter. The light on the floor at her feet dances on the hardwood so she can hardly keep her balance watching it. "I am the one who forgets," she says. "Not him."

As she says it, Gisela sinks. She sees the pewter coffee set still on the counter where she has left it, a dewdrop of milk still on the lip of the cream pitcher. She sees the window in the front room beyond Anne, and the ruffled buds of the plum tree she planted for Nils just outside it; the spread of sunlight on the planks of the hardwood beneath her like the water she poured in the bath earlier, and the small handful of crumbs Anne released onto the floor.

Gisela lets go her hold on the chair and feels Anne's hands firm beneath her back.

Annie looks away as she listens to Gisela. Yes, she thinks. That's right. You're right. He won't forget. There will be calls from the care center now, instead of from the house. There will be trips to the center in the dark when Gisela has a bad night, when she needs some little thing from the store—a bag of those lemon drops she loves, a new pair of slippers. Ben will be close enough for her to call and not feel she is imposing. Close enough for her to call, frantic, the first day she cannot remember where she is or why he's left her there. Of course she's right, Annie thinks. They will not be allowed to forget her now at all.

When her own mother was alive, there were days when she would call out for Annie from her bedroom, to bring her a sweater, to help her up to the bathroom, or find her a glass of water and an aspirin. "Anne," she would call, and Annie would turn away, ignoring at first. "Anne!" She called again, and Annie hummed to herself beneath her breath. But then, finally, her mother's voice rose and called out once more, impatient, but urgent enough to send a pulse of panic through Annie's body, to stop her from her playing and send her scrambling to get up the stairs, to get to her mother. Sometimes she dreams that panic now, still.

Annie looks to Gisela, begins to say again, aloud, "Yes, you're right, he won't ever forget you." But Gisela has closed her eyes. Her face has blanched, and Annie reaches out to her as she begins to sway on her feet. "Gisela?" Annie asks, but Gisela is going down.

Annie slides from her chair and slips her arms beneath Gisela's, catching her and easing her weight to the floor. Gisela's head is heavy in Annie's hands for just a moment, then her eyes open and she sits up.

"I saw you were going to fall," Annie says. She keeps her hands on Gisela's shoulders, and when Gisela shifts and turns toward her, Annie touches Gisela's forehead as she remembers touching her mother's, with the inside of her wrist, to feel for fever, or for chill. Her mother didn't like to be touched and always swatted her hand away, but Gisela does not. Gisela relaxes the back of her neck against Annie's forearm, allows the press of Annie's wrist. "You're just a little warm," Annie says, and braces her arms to help Gisela into her chair.

"I meant to walk," Gisela says.

"I know."

Gisela's braid has come loose at the nape of her neck, the tail of it hanging down her back, and she raises her hands to fix it.

"Let me," Annie says. She bends to collect the few fallen pins, then stands behind Gisela to begin re-pinning the braid.

"It happens," Gisela says, as Annie pushes the pins into place. "I know this is what happens."

Annie keeps one hand on Gisela's shoulder as she reworks the braid with the other. "Ben will be back soon," she says. "We'll have lunch when he gets here."

"He shouldn't have left you today," Gisela says. She turns her head to look at Annie. "We allow him too much. He's not a boy anymore."

Annie tucks the last loose strand into Gisela's braid. Still touching Gisela's shoulder, she pulls another chair close and sits down beside her.

The house is quiet around the two women. Neither of them speaks or moves. From where they sit, Annie can see the front room window, and the white, noon sunlight streaming in through its glass. The light seems to hold on to the walls of the house and to soak into the blond length of the floorboards. Annie is glad for its unfamiliar warmth, and the way it illumines the space. She takes her hand from Gisela's shoulder but does not get up. They can sit awhile longer, she thinks. They can wait together for Ben to return.

The House on the Lake

Otto rounded the corner and felt the tires of the van roll from the pavement onto the dirt road. The dirt was soft under the canopy of trees, covered in several winters' worth of cedar needles. It seemed to give a little beneath the van at first, to slow the movement of the tires, making Otto wonder if he should turn back around and forget about going to the house at all, pretend he had not received Ilsa's letter.

The house was forty-five years old, a wedding gift to them from Ilsa's parents. They had honeymooned there, and later brought their children every summer. The house was at the end of a long dirt road in the woods, tucked beneath the shade of an old-growth grove, facing the Selkirks and the lake. The nights they'd stayed there together, Otto was kept awake by the quiet lapping sound of the lake, and by the thick, inescapable scent of the cedars, which had at first been rich and enlivening, but over the years had come to remind him of the smell of an old and mothy closet, so that he felt cloistered, closed in.

When he'd received Ilsa's letter, inviting him to the house for the weekend, he left it opened on the tabletop for several days without responding. *The children will be up*, Ilsa had written in her tidy hand. She'd been training to be a school teacher when he met her, and though they'd married instead and she'd never taught, she had somehow kept up the pretty chalkboard penmanship. *Anton is bringing his boys, and Siri has asked her new someone to come as well,* she wrote. *They'd like to see you. It was Anton who gave me your address—he said he's had a postcard lately.* There was a space between one line and the next on the paper, and then her final sentence: *I have not told them about the separation.* She'd written her name at the bottom of the page, but above it no *Love* or *Best Regards* as a closing kindness.

Otto had been gone six months, and in that time had not spoken to his wife. He'd traveled. He'd been to state parks in Oregon and California first, then Colorado, South Dakota, Wyoming. There were mornings when he woke up, alone on the narrow mattress in the back of his van, and felt suddenly aware of Ilsa's absence, a feeling like stepping out of a warm, lit house onto an empty street at midnight. He felt like he could see the stars in a way he was sure he hadn't in the forty-two years they'd been together.

When the letter arrived, he'd been six weeks at a campground in Southern California, a place where the beach and the mountains met. There was the bittersweet smell of salt water and eucalyptus commingling, the morning fog climbing up the mountain side, and by evening, the clear view of the blue horizon line over the Pacific. The others at the campground called him "Swede," because of his name, he supposed, and the white fringe of short hair like a wreath around his head, and the unruly bristle of his red mustache. Nearly every afternoon he was invited to one or another of the motor homes parked along the beachfront, for a scotch and soda or a vodka martini, a game of rummy, or horseshoes in the pit beside the wash-house. "You've come all this way alone?" his host would finally ask. And Otto would nod, sip from his tumbler of scotch, and by his silence decline to explain further.

There were nights when he dreamed about her. Of course, he told himself when he woke, straightening, hardening himself against the onset of any loneliness, putting her out of his mind. Such dreams did not happen often, and had mostly to do with a sort of physical longing, a desire for her presence in the bed beside him, for which he did not chide himself. You can't be married to a woman forty-two years without a certain dependency, a certain and familiar need for her, he reasoned. And Ilsa was, even in her age, a lovely woman.

When he'd married her, she was a tall, slim girl, with hair redder than his, and legs like a track star's, thick with muscle. He liked to see her standing tiptoed at the counter in their first kitchen, reaching to the top shelves of the cupboards so that the winnowed lines in her calves stood out beneath the cropped legs of her pedal pushers. He moved up behind her then, kissed the bare back of her neck so that she startled, laughed, slapped at his hands, and pulled away from him. "There's dinner to get done," she would say, scolding until he left her.

He took her to a traveling carnival once, before the children, and at the end of the night there had been only enough tickets in his pocket for one of them to ride the Ferris wheel. He handed them to her, and she climbed into a chair by herself. She rode around and around, grinning and standing up in her seat when her chair reached the top, her bright hair wild with the breeze and catching the red and blue and white lights of the carnival below, the ruffled edge of her slip fluttering into sight as a gust of wind lifted her skirt above her knees.

She stepped off the ride breathless, and walked past him, so that he had to jog after her, and holler her name. "Oh!" she laughed, when she finally turned. "I forgot you were even down here!"

It was the way Ilsa had used the word *separation* in her letter that gave Otto pause, made him hesitate to head north again, to meet her and the children at the house. He had not quite thought of the six months he'd been away as a formal separation. He had not honestly thought of her much at all while he'd been gone, other than the dreams. In the evenings, sitting in the light of a camp lantern at the table he had rigged up in the back of the van, he laid out the faded road maps he carried, smoothed their folds with the flats of his hands, and looked over the tangled mess of pink and blue roads spread out before him. Otto liked the look of an open map, the strange and unplanned geometry of roads meeting and parting, meeting and parting. He imagined his traveling as a kind of unknotting of those roads in his mind. He kept a red pen in the front pocket of his flannel shirt, and as he ate his bowl of steamed rice or macaroni, he tagged the places he would like to see with a crisp check mark on the map. Each place he had seen he catalogued for himself, taking in and committing to memory the acrid taste of the air in Phoenix, the precise white of lightning as it struck the dirt in a North Dakota pasture, the Santa Barbara jacaranda trees in full, purple bloom. Marking these things he saw seemed a bigger kind of untangling, as if the threads of some self he had been knitting for years into a tight construction of knots were able to finally unravel. He was not certain that he had left Ilsa—not permanently—only that he was leaving that other disoriented and tangled self.

However, the way she'd written the word so firmly on the paper—*separation*—implied that Ilsa was certain.

The day he'd left, he had stood still in the drive a long time before actually going, looking at the van he'd loaded with a knapsack of clothes, a box of dry goods, a few books. They'd used the van for family vacations since the time the children were teenagers, twenty years at least, and the body looked worse for the wear. The paint job had been scratched here and there by bicycle handles and tent poles and slight brushes with trees. There was a dent in the back fender where Anton had backed into a fence the summer he had learned how to drive, and inside, a leaky back window they had never been able to fully repair. Otto had awakened that Sunday morning, the sound of Ilsa still breathing deeply with sleep beside him, the quiet emptiness of their house like a wide, white suggestion, and had simply decided to go.

"There are things I haven't seen," he explained to Ilsa, when she woke up to him packing. She sat in her nightgown in their bed, propped up against her pillow, her hair in a neat, red braid at her back. She had always slept with it braided that way, as long as he'd known her, to keep it from snarling, she'd said. She didn't like mess.

"So what?" she said. "There are things you have seen too."

Otto had made a trip out to the van already. He had settled a box into the back, and crawled up to sit in the driver's seat, to put his hands on the wheel. There he felt a space in front of him, suddenly, as if it had opened up in the night, the way a window opens, outward to the sky.

"I'm leaving today," he said.

He has not been able to remember if he asked her to come along, if she refused. Only that he got in the van that morning, and left.

Now, lumbering up the road to the lake house, he reached to pull from his head the wool cap he'd taken to wearing, then smoothed the fluff of his hair. He touched his fingers to his upper lip and brushed straight his mustache, dusted for crumbs of the doughnut he'd eaten that morning. He was not sure what she had told the children, since she hadn't called his absence a separation. He was not sure what lie he would need to adhere to in order to keep her from being the liar.

Once, when the children were still young, there had been a fight in the kitchen, a disagreement, which had ended with Ilsa throwing a can of stewed tomatoes at the kitchen wall. Their son appeared at the back door just as the hole had been made, and he looked with wide eyes at the white drywall dust on the kitchen tiles, the damaged wall. Ilsa's face flushed, and she looked to Otto. "Irresponsible," Otto said. He met Anton's stare. "Go find me the broom," he said to the boy, "so I can clean up this mess I've made."

That night, climbing into bed with their backs to each other, Ilsa reached up to turn out the light on the bed stand. "Thank you," she said, once it was dark. Otto did not answer but turned over, laid his hand on her hip, and fell asleep.

In the van, Otto took in a long breath and let it out between his teeth as the house came into view at the end of the road. It had not changed, and he felt both relieved and irritated to see the same, dark, mossy green of the old shingles, the door he'd painted red as a young man, the bramble of huckleberry bushes they'd allowed to grow wild over the years around the perimeter of the house. He stopped the van, smoothed the front of his shirt, got out.

Ilsa had sent Anton's boys out to pick huckleberries, and so had the house to herself. Anton and Siri and the restless, silent young man Siri had brought home had all gone into town for the day. "Go see a movie," Ilsa had said to them that morning at the breakfast table. She leaned over Anton's shoulder to slide another sausage onto his plate, whispered, "Have a drink at the bar." She wouldn't mind watching the boys, she told them, so that they could have some peace. But it was she who wanted the rest. She hadn't had both of her children in one place since the holidays, and there was something unquieting about it now, the crowd of people in the little lake house she'd grown accustomed to keeping alone in the past few months, the presence of Siri's beau.

"I want to know what you think of him, Mom," Siri had said. She and Ilsa had sat together on the porch the night before, once the boys were in bed and the two men were settled into a game of chess at the kitchen table. Ilsa had made tea, and they sat rocking in the old chairs Otto had built from a kit one summer. The chairs had become rickety, their wood stained with age and rotted soft in some places, but they could still hold weight.

Ilsa moved the soles of her bare feet back and forth across the tops of the porch boards as she rocked. The sound was like crinolines, she thought, the same rough brushing. "He doesn't say enough," Ilsa said. She lifted her tea to her mouth, let the steam cloud her vision of the shadowed cedar boughs beyond the porch, the flat sheen of the lake beyond that.

In truth, the young man reminded her too much of Otto. He will have secrets, she wanted to warn her daughter. One day you'll wake up and find you've only known his face, never his mind. She reached to touch Siri's hand, held it a moment, and let go.

She had decided when Otto left not to tell the children about it. Let Otto do it, she thought. He's an old man now. Let him explain his decisions. But instead of explaining himself, he sent postcards to Anton's boys from the places he stopped to camp, sent Siri glossy doubles of the photos he'd taken with the camera he'd charged to their credit card before Ilsa had the account number changed. On the backs of the postcards, Otto wrote travel notes and revised tourism slogans only he would find funny. *Tucson, AZ: temperate and dry. Piñon pines and mesquite. Jackrabbits and wild boar*, he wrote. Or, *The famed Mississippi, dirtiest river in the country. ~ Grandpa*

"Your father's having a vacation," Ilsa said over the phone when the children called. "Visiting old friends," she said. "He'll be home soon."

The children didn't ask after that. They didn't fuss over her when Ilsa packed up her things in the third month of Otto's absence and closed the house in Spokane, moved out to the lake.

It was the first time in her life that Ilsa had lived alone. There'd been her parents' house, and then the crowded college dorm of other girls, and then Otto. It was unsettling to begin with, the solitude. Perhaps, she thought, because it had not come as she'd expected. She'd expected that there would be a time without Otto at the end of her life, that he would pass first and leave her, as most wives are eventually left. Death, she thought, I could forgive him. Being left this way, however, the solitude made her angry, and nervous. The first night at the lake house, she'd moved through the dark rooms checking and rechecking the locks on the doors, the windows. She worked for twenty minutes to slide the bureau in front of the door, and then thought of things like fire and structural collapse, and had to shove it back, tossing all of Otto's old photographic equipment and fishing lures out of the drawers first, leaving them in a heap on the floor.

Finally, she got up at midnight one night and made hot chocolate from milk and sugar and a square of baking chocolate she found in the cupboard. She sat in the window seat and looked out at the black space she knew was the lake. Night was darker in the woods, and longer. She had not thought to bring a radio, and there was no television to turn on, no record player to create the illusion of other voices in the empty house. The quiet around her seemed to press and hum, and then, at some point during the night, to settle. Ilsa moved to the bedroom and lay down on the bed she was used to sharing with Otto, slid in beneath the blankets and slept. Habit broken, she thought, satisfied when she woke up rested the next day. He has been my habit.

After that, the solitude of the place only bothered her now and then. On long afternoons, when it seemed as if the silence might continue uninterrupted forever, Ilsa was unsure if the world beyond had fallen away, or if, perhaps, it was she who had disappeared. She walked along the soft path to the water and listened for the sound of her own footsteps landing but could hear nothing. I've been erased, she thought sometimes, and felt seized for an instant by fear. Other times the idea elated her, however, flooded her with relief. She'd been erased; she could begin again, someone new.

It was difficult not to think of her old life—of Otto—at all, though. The huckleberry bramble beyond the house was full, and each time she saw the berries she wished for one of Otto's pies. She'd always supervised the children in the berry picking, but Otto had better hands for making pastry, smooth and naturally cool skinned. His mother had taught him to roll dough so thin that when he slid the round of it from the floured countertop up into the pie dish, it would be translucent nearly, and unscarred by the tears and holes Ilsa's pie crusts tended to develop.

"You have to be patient," he told her once. He stood behind her, his hands over hers on the rolling pin, guiding. "You work too fast." His hands were cold. Each time he touched the dough, he dipped them into a bowl of ice water, to chill the skin so it wouldn't heat the lard, he said, turn the dough gummy. He leaned over her shoulder to see the dough then, and Ilsa kissed him twice along the rough, red line of whiskers at his jaw.

Swimming in the lake on warm afternoons, Ilsa sometimes imagined she saw his white head appear at the window of
the house, watching her as he often had. She scissored her legs a
moment, treading water and looking in a squint toward the house
before deciding that her eyes were making a fool of her. "I am a
ridiculous old woman," she said aloud, then slipped beneath the
black surface of the lake, shaking off the illusion, and swam back to
the dock.

The afternoon she wrote the letter, Ilsa thought she would
hang on to it awhile before sending it, decide if she really wanted
him at the house after all. It was June; the grandsons would be out
of school soon, and she had stopped in town that morning after buying groceries, made calls from a pay phone to invite Anton and Siri
out for the annual week's stay.

"Will Daddy be there?" Siri had asked.

"Of course," Ilsa said. The bag of groceries she'd been balancing on her hip had gotten heavy, and she stooped to set it at her
feet, pushed the bottle of wine she'd been holding in her other hand
down in beside the lettuce, the mini, half-dozen-sized carton of
eggs. "Your father will be here," she said. "He wouldn't miss it."

At the house that afternoon she wrote out the letter, choosing her words. She did not say she'd been living at the lake house
all spring, did not politely inquire about his travels, the people he'd
met. Ilsa did not say that she wanted him to come, only that the
children would be coming, that he was welcome to show up as well,
if he wished. *Our lives are going on, with or without you,* she meant
for him to understand. *You have not ruined us.*

She left the letter on the table for the night, and in the morning, printed her name in the corner, Otto's name in the center, above the Southern California address Anton had given her from his latest postcard. She drove into town and mailed it.

And then there was no word from him, no postcard even, to let her know he had received the letter. He has gone completely, Ilsa thought. She felt the idea begin to stiffen in her mind, like a stone, solid, gray, settled.

But when the children arrived, and Siri dropped her suitcase near the door and said, "I don't see Daddy's van," Ilsa reached out to hug her. "You beat him," she said. "I'm sure he's broken down somewhere, or left too late. You know your father." She released her daughter, walked off to begin a lunch for all of them.

Now, the children gone for the day, Ilsa stood at the window of the house and peered down at the blond heads of Anton's boys in the backyard. They had set their buckets down in the grass and were eating the berries as they picked them from the bramble. Beyond the boys, the lake was a plate of black glass, clear and placid and unshattered by the windless morning. It would be a pleasant week together at the lake, a pleasant summer. Ilsa turned and went to the door for her sweater. She opened the door and stepped out to join the boys.

Otto saw her from the road, standing on the stoop in front of the house, as if she had been waiting for him all this time. My Penelope, he thought, softening to her a moment. She had cut her hair close to her head, and it was whiter than he remembered, the red faded to a milky copper. Other than that, however, she looked much the same, tall, slender, unforgiving. Otto lifted his hand and waved.

Across the yard, Ilsa folded her arms over her body and stood still. For an instant, she believed she was imagining him again. But then he waved, and she saw more clearly the expression on his face, like fear, the way he hesitated when she didn't wave back. So, she thought, he's decided to make an appearance. She did not move but waited for him to walk down the stone path to the door toward her. He could come to her, after all.

When he reached the stoop, Otto stood a moment, then leaned to hug her. "Ilsa," he said, and put his arms around her, carefully, awkward as he would have been hugging another man's wife. "You look well." He nodded to her head. "I like what you've done to your hair."

"Thank you," she said, without taking her eyes from him. He smelled of an unfamiliar sort of soap, not the kind Ilsa had always bought, and of the aftershave he'd worn since she'd met him. "I suppose what matters is that I like it," she said. She had not smiled, had not unfolded her arms from her chest, and she stood in front of the door firmly, the huckleberry bucket she'd picked up to take down to the boys still in her hand.

Somewhere off behind the house, Otto could hear his grandsons' voices, and there was the press of the lake smell he had expected in the air, the mineral scent of the water, the brown, uncomfortable scent of things decomposing at the shore line, becoming mud. Above him, the cedars dripped and hid the sun.

He shifted his weight from one foot to the other. Fine, he thought. He raised his eyes to Ilsa's, nodded. You've won.

She felt herself ease then, and turned, moved into the house. "The older ones have gone for the day, only the boys are here," she said. "I have coffee going. I'll get you some." She walked to the kitchen and heard the front door close as he followed her into the house.

Otto waited for her in the front room. The house looked more lived-in than he'd ever seen it, homier. There was a pile of blankets on the window seat across the living room, afghans and quilts Otto recognized from the Spokane house. The pillows she'd embroidered for that other house were there, on the old chairs, and the photograph she'd kept above the fireplace of the children when they were young had been moved as well and hung over this mantel.

"You've always talked about retiring here," Otto said. He turned when Ilsa came in from the kitchen and took the coffee she offered him. She'd put cream in it, he noticed, just as he liked it.

"I don't know if this is retirement," Ilsa said. "I've just come up here for a while." She crossed the room and sat down on the window seat, folding her left leg beneath her. It was a familiar movement, graceful, and Otto wondered how long it would take for her body to become foreign to him, or if he would always know her that way, always know her movements, the shape of her walking into the room, because she'd been like an extension of his own body to him for so many years. She set her coffee cup on the window ledge, looked down. "Anton's boys are picking berries," she said, and looked back to Otto. She smiled. "They've grown. You're missing that."

Otto put his palms around his cup. He recognized it as one of the mugs Siri or Anton had made in high school, thrown on a potter's wheel in art class. It was lopsided, the ceramic lumpy and the glaze uneven. It was difficult to drink from without dribbling. "I have photos in the van," he said. "Grand Canyon and that place I've been staying in California, on the beach. I should bring them in a little later, show you what I've been seeing."

"We went to the Grand Canyon," Ilsa said. "We went when Siri was small. You hated it. I remember that. Anton got sick to his stomach in the tent, and you said we'd never go back. 'It looks just like the postcard,' you said." She looked to him. "I remember you saying that."

"We couldn't hike down at all," Otto said. He felt warm beneath his shirt, behind his eyes, as if the coffee had been too strong, or he hadn't slept enough the night before. Warm and tired. He reached up to rub the back of his neck. "We couldn't get down to the river with the children."

"Yes," Ilsa said. "A family can get in the way." She watched him get up and walk to the other window, to see the boys below. He looked older, like an old man, and she wondered if it was the distance that made her see it, or if he had really aged without her, if the months he'd been away had been hard on him, had whitened his hair even more. Now that he was in the room with her again, she could imagine him all those evenings in the van, and in spite of herself, she felt a swell of pity for him, for herself.

"Of course I don't mean it like that," Otto said. He crossed the room again, picked up a pinecone one of the boys had found and set on the mantel, examined it, put it down.

"Why don't you sit," Ilsa said. "You're like a caged bird in here. I wouldn't think it'd be that bad."

"I'm reacquainting myself. You've changed things."

"I don't think that was me." Ilsa watched him choose a chair, adjust the pillows she'd brought from the other house, sit back. He had become persnickety in his solitude; without her, he had become one of those particular old men, the kind who carry peppermints in their pockets and tidy their mustaches in the mornings with tiny combs. She pressed her lips together, did not grin.

Otto looked up at her, serious. "You've been all right?" he asked.

"This house is not so uncomfortable as we thought all those years."

"You've been comfortable then?"

"I have running water. You," Ilsa began, "have that van." She turned her face away from him, toward the window, where a thin band of sunlight was reflecting off the lake and hitting the glass. It lit her hair, and he saw her there as a young woman, sitting in that window at noon, her red hair all in flames. *The burning bush*, he used to joke, and she would toss a pillow at him, put her hands to her head in embarrassment.

"Ilsa," he said, "I want to know how you've been."

Below the window, Ilsa watched the boys chasing each other up and down the length of the yard. Their arms and shirts were blotched with stains from the berries they'd begun to throw at each other. She stood up. "Those boys have eaten enough berries to fill three pies this morning," she said, and moved past Otto toward the kitchen. "It's nearly noon. I should get them some sandwiches before they make themselves sick."

In the kitchen, Ilsa laid out eight slices of bread on the countertop, opened the icebox, and bent to find the tomatoes, the cheese, an apple to slice for the boys. She could hear Otto in the other room, up again and wandering, looking at the place as if it were a museum, as if he hadn't spent every summer since he was twenty-five sitting in that very chair, looking out at the lake. She didn't want him to ask how she'd been, to have to tell him. It was exhausting. How long had they known everything together, at once, as if they'd inhabited a shared and singular life? Now he moved inside her house like a friendly stranger.

A visitor, Ilsa said to herself as she stood at the sink and washed an apple. I'm too old to be a good hostess now, she thought. Too comfortable alone. She picked up the paring knife, skinned the peel from the apple.

Otto crossed the house to stand at the kitchen door, watched her peel the apple. "I've always been impressed by that," he said. He smiled as she held up the long curl of apple peel for him so that it stretched, then she stooped to toss it into the trash.

"It's not that difficult," Ilsa said. She looked down, cut the apple into slices.

Otto stood at the counter as she worked. He was not sure if he had missed this, the daily rituals, the breakfasts and lunches and dinners spent together at the table. He tried to imagine himself later that evening, his children and his grandchildren beside him at the table. He would be called upon to say grace, as always, and he would say it just as he had every night forever. Come, Lord Jesus, he would say. Be our guest. And let these gifts to us be blest. But he would feel the guest.

In the other room, he had stood among their things, his and Ilsa's, the furniture he'd built as a young man, the quilts and trinkets and books he recognized as gifts for anniversaries and births and graduation days, the family photographs on the shelves of the bookcase and the mantel. Otto felt little more for these things than nostalgia, a kind of pink and familiar fondness, a fading attachment. He had gone to the window and looked down at his grandsons, with their heads of hair as white-blond as their father's had once been, and he had felt love, yes, but grandfatherly love, love relieved of obligation, released to stand at a distance. His children were grown. He had done well by them. He had done his job.

Otto watched as Ilsa moved to the cupboard, reached up for the plates, and then, higher, to the top shelf for a glass dish. She stood on tiptoe, arched up, and he remembered the lovely curve of her back, the line of her. He watched as her fingers felt for the dish and then found it and nudged it toward the edge of the shelf, and her other opened hand. It was too much a reach for her; the dish would fall, he could see. "Let me get it," Otto said suddenly, too loud. He lunged toward her so that Ilsa startled and turned to look at him, lifted her hand from the dish.

The dish tipped from the shelf and fell, smashed on the tiles at their feet. Bits of glass sparkled up at them from between the tiles, glittered against the dark grout.

"Please," Ilsa said. Otto had grabbed her arm, and she stepped away from his hold. "Please. I'm fine. I should have seen it coming." Her face was warm, and she reached up, touched her hair, straightened herself. Otto was still close to her, his hand at her elbow. She had felt his breath on her neck for a moment, before she pulled away. "Thank you," she said. And then, in a certain voice, "I'm just fine." She took his hand from her arm, held it a moment, let go.

At the window, the light moved with the breeze, splitting with the shadows of the tree boughs, then splitting again, so that the window glass and ledge were freckled instead of fully lit, dappled with the shifting fragments of sun.

Otto nodded and stepped back. "Let me clean it up then," he said. He went to the closet near the icebox, got out the broom and pan, and swept up the glass.

Ilsa moved to the table, set the boys' sandwiches at their places, and bent to fold the napkins into triangles, laid them beside the plates. "Will you be staying for lunch?" she asked.

Otto shook his head, and Ilsa turned and opened a drawer, took out a roll of waxed paper, and wrapped his sandwich.

"That's fine," she said. "I'd rather you weren't here when the boys come up then." She set his sandwich at the empty place on the table. "It will stir them up if they see you, and I'd rather have a quiet afternoon."

Otto looked up at her for a moment. "I will call Anton and Siri," he said. "When I stop somewhere for a few days. You can tell them to expect my call." He kneeled and picked the last shards of glass up with his fingertips, careful, then stood and emptied the dustpan into the trash. "It was a pretty dish," he said.

Ilsa turned, the table set, and met his eyes. "These things happen." She went to the door and opened it. "I'll meet you outside," she said, and stepped out.

On the stoop, the air was cool. She would go for a swim later, she thought, once the children returned. She had never swum all the way across the lake, to the pebbled beach on the other side, and it seemed a good day to do that, no rain clouds threatening an afternoon storm, and the water so calm.

Ilsa crossed her arms over her chest, looked out at the yard, the square of mud and weeds before the road. She had been meaning to come out with her clippers since coming to the lake. The huckleberry bramble had not been cut back in several years, and it looked a mess there against the house, a wild, discouraging tangle. Looking at it now, though, she thought it might wait. She had time. She had a whole summer ahead of her.

Inside, Otto picked up his sandwich and followed Ilsa out of the house. He put his hand to her back when he reached her, leaned forward to kiss her cheek, and walked out toward the road. At the van, he climbed into his seat and turned on the motor. He was not certain where he would go once he found the highway again. He would have to stop for the night somewhere nearby, take out his maps, decide on a new direction, it didn't matter which one.

As he pulled the van around, Otto rolled down the window, lifted his hand to wave. He watched Ilsa raise her hand as well, watched her finally turn and disappear into the house before he started off. He wanted to remember her this way now when he thought of home, Ilsa here beside the wide shine of the lake, beneath the sky of cedars with their green and stinging smell. How was it she had described that scent so many years ago, the first time they'd come out to the lake? *Like suitcase sachets*, she'd said, taking his hand and then releasing it. *Like a hope chest opened up.*